DEVIL DADDY

JOHN BLACKBURN

I0524474

VALANCOURT BOOKS

Devil Daddy by John Blackburn
First published London: Jonathan Cape, 1972
First Valancourt Books edition 2015

Published by Valancourt Books, Richmond, Virginia
http://www.valancourtbooks.com

All Valancourt Books publications are printed on acid free paper that meets all ANSI standards for archival quality paper.

ISBN 978-1-941147-76-4 (*trade paperback*)

Set in Dante MT 10.5/12.6
Cover by Lorenzo Princi

DEVIL DADDY

JOHN BLACKBURN was born in 1923 in the village of Corbridge, England, the second son of a clergyman. Blackburn attended Haileybury College near London beginning in 1937, but his education was interrupted by the onset of World War II; the shadow of the war, and that of Nazi Germany, would later play a role in many of his works. He served as a radio officer during the war in the Mercantile Marine from 1942 to 1945, and resumed his education afterwards at Durham University, earning his bachelor's degree in 1949. Blackburn taught for several years after that, first in London and then in Berlin, and married Joan Mary Clift in 1950. Returning to London in 1952, he took over the management of Red Lion Books.

It was there that Blackburn began writing, and the immediate success in 1958 of his first novel, *A Scent of New-Mown Hay*, led him to take up a career as a writer full time. He and his wife also maintained an antiquarian bookstore, a secondary career that would inform some of Blackburn's work, including the bibliomystery *Blue Octavo* (1963). *A Scent of New-Mown Hay* typified the approach that would come to characterize Blackburn's twenty-eight novels, which defied easy categorization in their unique and compelling mixture of the genres of science fiction, horror, mystery, and thriller. Many of Blackburn's best novels came in the late 1960s and early 1970s, with a string of successes that included the classics *A Ring of Roses* (1965), *Children of the Night* (1966), *Nothing but the Night* (1968; adapted for a 1973 film starring Christopher Lee and Peter Cushing), *Devil Daddy* (1972) and *Our Lady of Pain* (1974). Somewhat unusually for a popular horror writer, Blackburn's novels were not only successful with the reading public but also won widespread critical acclaim: the *Times Literary Supplement* declared him 'today's master of horror' and compared him with the Grimm Brothers, while the *Penguin Encyclopedia of Horror and the Supernatural* regarded him as 'certainly the best British novelist in his field' and the *St James Guide to Crime & Mystery Writers* called him 'one of England's best practicing novelists in the tradition of the thriller novel'.

By the time Blackburn published his final novel in 1985, much of his work was already out of print, an inexplicable neglect that continued until Valancourt began republishing his novels in 2013. John Blackburn died in 1993.

By John Blackburn

A Scent of New-Mown Hay (1958)*
A Sour Apple Tree (1958)
Broken Boy (1959)*
Dead Man Running (1960)
The Gaunt Woman (1962)
Blue Octavo (1963)*
Colonel Bogus (1964)
The Winds of Midnight (1964)
A Ring of Roses (1965)*
Children of the Night (1966)*
The Flame and the Wind (1967)*
Nothing but the Night (1968)*
The Young Man from Lima (1968)
Bury Him Darkly (1969)*
Blow the House Down (1970)
The Household Traitors (1971)*
Devil Daddy (1972)*
For Fear of Little Men (1972)
Deep Among the Dead Men (1973)
Our Lady of Pain (1974)*
Mister Brown's Bodies (1975)
The Face of the Lion (1976)*
The Cyclops Goblet (1977)*
Dead Man's Handle (1978)
The Sins of the Father (1979)
A Beastly Business (1982)*
The Book of the Dead (1984)
The Bad Penny (1985)*

* Available or forthcoming from Valancourt Books

'Tell us where you got your lessons and you shall have it,' said I. 'Who's your master?'
'Devil daddy,' was his answer.

Ellen Dean in *Wuthering Heights*

Prologue

'I have told you what I experienced and repeat that the instructions were as clear to me as if one of you had just voiced them.' The man was addressing a tense and very oddly assorted audience. No butcher or baker or candlestick maker was present, but his listeners included a mechanic and a millionaire, a bank manager and a photographer, a doctor of medicine and a manservant, a very old, very staid lady in a wheelchair and a blowsy suburban housewife with glaring auburn hair and thick scarlet lipstick smeared across her mouth like sealing-wax on a parcel.

'My dream ... my vision, as I believe the phenomenon to be, came to me after years of study, it is supported by historical records, and I beg ... I implore you to act upon the orders given to me. If this person is the one I suspect him to be ... if I was not deluded by wishful thinking, he could be of vital use to our organization, and no time should be lost.' The speaker was a clergyman. He wore a formal black suit and a white dog-collar, and his surroundings were brown. A brown carpet covered the floor, the walls were panelled in oak, and russet curtains draped the windows. The table he sat at was mahogany, parchment-shaded lamps glinted on the brown leather bindings in a bookcase behind him and smoke had laid an ochre patina on the ceiling. The room smelled of brown sherry, tobacco and the acrid sweat of excited human beings.

'I emphasize the need for speed. As you know, the man is a traveller who rarely remains long in one place, so please ... please accept the possibility that I am correct and act now. At least examine the case and prove me right or wrong.' He leaned back and waited for their decision, his body tense as the sounds of hesitation drifted around him. The scrape of a match – a cough – a click as the housewife opened her powder compact – the drumming of the bank manager's fingers on the table top. Finally the judgment.

'We have no choice, in my view.' The millionaire industrialist

often presided at board meetings and he enjoyed swaying opinions; moreover, before entering commerce, he had been an army
officer and fancied himself as a strategist. 'If there is the slightest
chance that the story is factual and the man is what you say, we
must naturally act upon your belief, and act quickly.

'But also act methodically, and I shall ask you, Mr Stephenson,
to provide us with visual records of our progress.' The industrialist nodded at the photographer, and then scowled up and down
the table to challenge a dissension.

'No, no risk is too great in view of the possible benefits, and
the findings of our host seem to support what Canon Hamilton
has told us.' He bowed gravely to a man facing him. 'And so that
time is not wasted, I suggest that the evidence should be tested
within the next few days, and there is a very simple way to do
that.' His eyes softened, the scowl crinkled into a smile and the
domineering voice became cynical.

'We shall kill this person, ladies and gentlemen . . . or rather,
try to kill him.'

One

'Mr Batterday does a little private dealing in pictures, he sometimes illustrates children's books, but most important of all, he
might be regarded as an escapologist.' Professor Herbert Henson
checked the catch of his safety belt while he spoke. He was a
nervous man, and in his opinion the car was travelling far too
fast. 'Yes, I think I may have seen some of his illustrations. Rather
amusing little watercolours in which animals have human char-
acters and trades; Mr Rat, the miner, with a great scaly tail poking
out through his baggy breeches – that sort of thing.' The professor chuckled, though he felt far from happy, and he clutched the
door handle to steady himself as the Ferrari hurtled towards a
junction.

'However, in private Mr Batterday prefers another school of
art and he is also well acquainted with the last enemy. Interesting,
Tania. Very interesting indeed, so let us hope and pray that he
will be prepared to talk frankly about his experiences.

'But do have a care, my dear.' Henson's foot came down on an imaginary brake pedal as his driver swung the wheel hard over to the left. Lady Tania Levin belonged to a growing school of women motorists who consider that cut and thrust provides the shortest route between two points and she had shot into the main road, gracefully saluting an enraged taxi driver as though believing he had intended to give way for her. 'Apart from our own safety, this car must have cost your good gentleman a great deal of money.'

'Over ten thousand pounds. But not to worry; Mark can well afford it.' Tania smiled proprietorially at the gleaming bonnet. She was a fair-haired girl with a statuesque figure which contrasted with a soulful, oval-shaped face as though the Venus de Milo had joined forces with a pre-Raphaelite madonna. 'And time's getting on, you know. I told John we'd be with him by eleven.'

'So you said, but surely a few minutes won't matter, and though I am eager to meet Mr Batterday, more haste, less speed is a sound maxim.' The professor gave an agonized gasp. Tania had failed to beat a traffic light and her sudden application of the brakes had jerked him painfully against the belt.

'As you can see, that same last enemy is always hard at work.' He nodded at a line of newspaper placards on the pavement: MULTIPLE PILE-UP ON MOTORWAY; NORTH SEA DISASTER – HEAVY LOSS OF LIFE; EARTHQUAKE DEATH-ROLL MOUNTS. 'Though I am a seeker after spiritual truth, survival in this world has some importance.'

'It is also the reason for your interest in John Batterday, Herbert.' Tania was waiting impatiently for the lights to change. 'Have you worked out a line of questioning?'

'Not yet, my dear. I want to study him first, to watch his face and try to feel the man's aura.' Henson lit a cigarette to steady his nerves. He was short and stout and middle-aged, with a pompous, academic manner and a shock of unruly grey hair that arched over his forehead as though he were a circus performer riding a motor-cycle backwards.

'What a fascinating subject survival is, and your Mark might also be described as one of its supreme examples, Tania. Sir Marcus Levin, Knight Companion of the Bath, Fellow of the

Royal Society, the winner of a Nobel Prize for services to medicine, and generally recognized as one of the world's foremost bacteriologists.' The light had turned to green, but the traffic was at a crawl and there seemed little chance that Tania could pass the lorry in front of them. Henson relaxed slightly.

'Yes, Mark is an eminent and successful man at the height of his career, but what agonies he must have suffered in his youth. Does he ever talk to you about the past? "Those old, unhappy far-off times and battles long ago." '

'Very rarely.' Tania frowned irritably. Like her husband, the professor had an annoying habit of bringing out quotations she had never heard of. Though the words were appropriate, of course. Mark Levin was an eminent man, but he had been born Marcus Levinski, the son of a small Polish shopkeeper, and his early life had certainly contained unhappy times. Mark was also a supreme survivor, as Henson had said. He had experienced the battle of the Warsaw Ghetto, the Ruhr labour camps and Belsen.

'I think Mark has deliberately tried to strip the past from his mind. Mainly because he believes in forgiveness of one's enemies, and the war ended a long time ago. Also because . . .' Tania paused. There was another reason, but she wasn't going to discuss it with Henson; a man whose interests she shared, but with whom she never felt completely at ease. 'Because the memories naturally distress him.'

That was true enough, she thought, but the other reason was not so natural or innocent. Mark worshipped success and despised failure and he no longer felt any kinship with the child who had cowered in the Warsaw rubble – no communion with the penniless refugee who had arrived in England praying that one day a British medical school would accept him. Though Tania was deeply in love with her husband, she did not number modesty among his virtues and she knew that he had rejected his past because it was a story of defeat and best forgotten. Mark had his title and his Nobel Prize and a job that fascinated him. He had money in the bank, the respect of people whose opinions he valued and, though she said it herself, he had an extremely happy marriage. There was no place for a waif named Marcus Davuidov Levinski in such successful surroundings.

'How can I explain, Herbert?' Tania judged the gap between the lorry and the oncoming traffic as she spoke. 'On the rare occasions that Mark does talk about his early life, it's rather as if he were describing events that happened to somebody else. That he'd read about or heard repeated by another person.'

'I see. An attempt at dismissal ... mental withdrawal from suffering.' Henson pulled at his cigarette. He and Mark Levin met at St Bede's Hospital from time to time, but they were not close friends. In fact he suspected that Mark disapproved of him and resented his association with Tania, and his suspicions were correct. The professor was a psychiatrist, and as a bacteriologist dealing with material causes and effects, Mark distrusted the profession in general. Worse than that, Henson was also a keen student of the occult and one of the joint editors of a magazine called the *Psychic Observer*. In Mark's opinion its contents were largely composed of pretentious mumbo-jumbo, but the subject fascinated Tania and she had struck up an acquaintanceship with Henson on the strength of it. To gain copy for the *Observer* was the reason for their present journey.

'But though Mark tries to lock out suffering, let us hope that our quarry has preserved a more troubled memory.' Henson's foot pressure increased as Tania grasped 'this nettle danger' firmly and accelerated between the lorry and an approaching bus, missing both by inches. 'Batterday – John Batterday; an unusual name. I missed the significance at first and thought it was of North Country origin; Yorkshire perhaps.'

'What significance, Herbert?' Tania took her eyes off the road and glanced at him. 'I'm not with you.'

'Nothing important, my dear.' The professor sounded slightly guarded. 'Just that you told me Batterday, like Mark, was a Jewish refugee, so the name was probably adopted because it resembled some German original. The significant things are the man's taste in art and the experiences he has gone through. Do you think he will be prepared to talk about them frankly?'

'I honestly haven't a clue, Herbert.' Tania had been married for six years, but she was a Soviet citizen when Mark and she first met and her Russian accent clashed attractively with the jargon of the English middle class.

'Before you showed me those clippings I knew very little about John's background. He's an interesting man and an extraordinarily well-educated one; he and Mark can discuss medicine on pretty equal terms and he knows a damn sight more Russian history than I do. But he's pretty reticent about himself and though we've been to his house and he to ours a couple of times, you can't say it's an intimate relationship. On the whole we just chat about generalities; mainly art and so forth. In fact, if it wasn't for his physical appearance we'd have very little in common.'

Tania fell silent, recalling her first encounter with John Batterday. She and Mark had been shopping in Bond Street and a Brueghel reproduction in a small art gallery had attracted their attention. Another potential customer was examining a picture by the door when they entered and he had stepped aside to let them pass, smiling politely as he did so. Starting to smile that was. As he looked at Mark the smile had been stripped from the man's face, his eyes had widened in recognition and his mouth gaped open. The Levins had responded in exactly the same way and for perhaps ten seconds the three had stood staring at each other too astounded to speak. That first surprise had formed their acquaintanceship and it had persisted over the months. Tania knew that when she and Henson reached Batterday's house, his appearance would shock her as strongly as ever.

'You discuss art with him. Yes, you told me that Mark was fascinated by his collection, Tania.' The car had turned into a quiet side street and Henson's foot left the imaginary pedal. 'At first he thought the pictures were originals. Uncatalogued masterpieces by Bosch, Callot, Cranach, etcetera.'

'Only for a moment. As soon as Mark thought he'd spotted a Dürer, the penny dropped and we knew they were all contemporary copies, competent works by imitators and students of the same schools. Probably worth a lot of money, but if they were originals they'd be priceless. John would need security guards and a pack of alsatian dogs to protect them.'

'Naturally, but it's the subject matter that interests me, and what a stroke of luck that you know the man.' The professor drew a wad of newspaper clippings from his pocket. 'When the press cutting agency sent us back references of psychic phenomena recorded over the last five years, I couldn't gather why these were included. But when the light dawned I became so eager to meet Mr Batterday, and finally, just the other day, you casually mentioned the name. And now you are taking me to meet him.' The professor smiled at the records of long-forgotten news.

'Yes, it all fits. Bosch – Callot – Cranach – Dürer, and other artists who were morbidly obsessed with death, evil and hellfire. That is the kind of work Mr Batterday treasures, and I believe I know why.' He thumbed on through the clippings, nodding from time to time. 'On at least three occasions the curtain was lifted for John Batterday and he must have experienced something very strange indeed. He is bound to have felt the actual touch of the reaper's scythe and he won't have cast off his experiences as Mark tries to do. Mark was not alone during his sufferings, remember, and he was only a boy. The young cannot visualize death, and they are resilient. However bad things might be, Mark would have believed he'd come through them. That the Red Army would advance on Warsaw and save the ghetto . . . that he would endure the concentration camp till the Allies arrived – as indeed he did.' Henson had re-read the last sheet of typescript and he tucked away the clippings.

'But Batterday was not a young man when his sufferings occurred and he had no companions to share them. For lengthy periods of time he must have been completely without hope and felt sure that he was about to die. And isn't it possible that he did die . . . that for a brief instant he entered the actual state of death?' The professor's excitement was mounting, his pompous manner had vanished and he sounded almost boyish. 'Yes, his taste in art suggests that to me. Charming little illustrations for children's stories on the one hand. Obscene imitations of medieval witch-hunters on the other.

'And if only . . . if only the man will be open with me. If only I can make him relive his experiences and describe them . . .' Henson had been talking as much to himself as to Tania, but now he turned to her and became practical. 'But Batterday will obviously find the memories distressing, and we must bring them up carefully. Remember that I'm merely a friend who is interested in bizarre forms of art, and let me introduce the subject.

You say that he's a reticent fellow, so I must play him like a fish.

'You don't mean this is where he lives?' Tania had parked behind a small van labelled RITE LITE PHOTOGRAPHIC SERVICES, and Henson raised his eyebrows at the trim suburban bungalow. All the houses in the road were newish and well-cared for, but Batterday shamed his neighbours with Snowcemmed walls, gleaming white paint and a lawn that looked like a seedsman's advertisement. 'I know the area slightly, but I never imagined anything like this. So smug . . . so ordinary . . . so "keeping up with the Joneses". And when one thinks what its owner has gone through.'

'What did you expect, Herbert? A moated grange, or Castle Dracula with film-set gargoyles?' Tania stepped out of the car. 'However, don't let first impressions deceive you. The inside is chilling enough, I promise.' Their arrival had been noticed, a hand had waved from a window and she led the way forward up the gravel path, bracing herself for the astonishment she knew she would experience when the door opened. As usual it was forthcoming.

Marcus Levin was a distinguished-looking man and John Batterday was not. Mark dressed the part, always wearing gloves in the street, and his beautifully cut suits cost him a hundred guineas a time. The man who opened the door wore gloves, but they were to hide disfiguring scars and, though his suit was clean and well-pressed, it had been bought off the peg and was a little too tight around the waist.

Mark Levin's manner was jaunty and assured and he radiated professional confidence. When he entered a sickroom one could almost read the nurses' thoughts. 'Sir Marcus has arrived, so stop worrying.' 'The crisis is over because the specialist has taken charge.' John Batterday's manner hinted at nervous tension, worry and lack of self-confidence. Mark's hair was short – Batterday's was long. Mark usually held himself erect – Batterday's shoulders slumped.

Where dress and bearing were concerned the two men had nothing in common. But the flesh was their bond and 'as like as two peas' was an accurate cliché to describe their features. While

Tania watched her host smile down from the doorway she felt
that she was seeing her husband's face reflected in a glass.

Two

'Fascinating, Mr Batterday ... quite fascinating.' Henson had
stood silently in the doorway of the little art gallery as if too intrigued to speak, but now he put on his spectacles and hurried
forward. The room was lit by ceiling lamps that blazed down on
the exhibits causing some of them to glow as though the paint
was phosphorous and produced a light of its own.

'I shall never forget this first sight of your collection, sir.' The
professor had adopted the role of art connoisseur to gain Batterday's confidence, but the gallery's contrast to the rest of the
house had clearly surprised him as much as it had done Tania and
Mark on an earlier visit. Like its exterior, the inside of the bungalow was bright and recently decorated and John Batterday's own
works hung in the hall and corridors. Mother rabbits in Victorian
gowns, a fox with a monocle and a cigar stuck in his overshot
jowl, Old Farmer Brock, the badger, weeding his cabbage patch.
Pleasant studies on the lines of Beatrix Potter, but they did very
little to give the building character or make it a home. The paintwork was too bright, the furniture too functional; fumed oak and
stainless steel; everything was stark and ordered and over-clean.
Batterday did not employ a housekeeper or even a daily woman,
but the whole house looked as though it had just been dusted and
polished and the effect was as antiseptic as an operating theatre;
as dead and depressing as a morgue. Only the art gallery contained life and that was of a very disturbing sort.

'Yes indeed. Lady Levin was right in saying you had interesting
tastes.' The professor leaned back against a table, peering at the
largest canvas, a vast study of a cave with a group of outlandish
creatures huddled around a fire. Their faces and bodies were half-
human, half-animal and all of them were utterly repulsive.

'A fantasy inspired by the beasts of St John's *Revelation* I presume ... Mr ... Mr Batterday.' For some reason Henson hesitated
over the name. 'And executed in the manner of Hieronymus

Bosch. Most impressive, and if I hadn't been forewarned I might
have considered it an original Bosch.'

'Hardly that, Professor.' John Batterday had no accent to speak
of, and like his house his voice was strangely lifeless. Sad too:
his whole personality emanated sadness, and as always happened
when she was with him Tania's sympathies were aroused. She
had wanted children, an accident had deprived her of the chance
to ever have a child, but her maternal instincts remained and at
the moment they were directed on Batterday. He was as old as
her husband, probably a little older, but he was such an unhappy
man. An atmosphere of defeat and resignation continually surrounded him and she was sure that it had not been caused by the
events described in Henson's press cuttings. People shrug off the
memory of past dangers, as Mark had done, and physical pain
is soon forgotten. 'Bad times – good times – all times pass over,'
was a favourite maxim of Mark's and he had certainly cast aside
his experiences. But Tania had a notion that in John Batterday's
past there had been an event which would always haunt him. Not
something that had been done to him, but a happening in which
he had been actively involved or had even instigated. An incident
that would haunt his memory for eternity.

Eternity! A myth, Tania thought to herself. Though she took a
keen interest in the possibility of a spiritual world she didn't really
believe in one. The last enemy, the reaper, as Henson pompously
called death, was always on hand to give peace, and no god would
be cruel enough to condemn his creatures to everlasting life. She
pushed the notion aside and listened to the conversation.

'Yes, naturally a copy, though an astonishingly fine one.'
Henson had left the table and was craning forward over the
big canvas. 'Though I'm rather sorry that the Great Whore of
Babylon is so unappetizing. In real life she was probably a very
pretty girl.' He squinted at a detail in the left-hand corner of the
picture. 'And who is this? Some shadowy third person standing in
the entrance of the pit who seems both intrigued and repelled by
the gathering.

'Now what have we here?' He turned to the next exhibit, a
copperplate engraving. 'No date, signature or title, but surely . . .
surely it's a Dürer? The style is unmistakable and so is the whole

composition. Notice the similarity to his famous *The Knight, Death and the Devil.*'

'Merely a skilful imitation, Professor.' Batterday was at Henson's side, and now that his back was towards her, Tania saw that all resemblance to Mark had vanished. The two men's stances were quite different and only their faces tallied. She also noticed that tension had joined Batterday's usual aura of sadness and he seemed to be on his guard. Was it possible that he had guessed the true reason for their visit and resented it? 'Perhaps it is by a student of Dürer, but certainly not by the master himself.'

'I must accept your word, Mr ... Mr Batterday.' The professor hesitated over the name a second time. 'A very fine piece of work, however, and I wonder what the title should be. We have a pack of hounds in charge of a single huntsman and their prey is just visible beyond that thicket; maybe a boar or a small stag.' He polished his glasses, replaced them and frowned. 'No, the quarry is human, an exhausted man or woman crawling on hands and knees. Which shows that the location is Bavaria, France or Windsor Great Park. That the rider is Herne; the victim, doomed humanity; and a Wild Hunt is in progress.

'Yes, all quite fascinating, and I am most grateful for the privilege of viewing your treasures.' Henson moved slowly around the walls nodding and clicking his teeth in enthusiasm, but Tania suspected that some of the works disturbed him. 'Another one lacking a date, title or signature, but it's obviously sixteenth-century Dutch or German and the artist followed the schools of Grünewald and Lucas Cranach.' He stooped to examine a second engraving.

'The subject matter is apparent enough. Christ mocked and buffeted on the Road to Calvary. Strange how Jesus is portrayed as small and insignificant; only recognizable by the cross, while the chief of his tormentors towers over him.' Henson pointed to a tall man brandishing a club. 'And in the background – far up on the slopes of Golgotha there is an observer. A person with horns.

'Do you believe the devil is like that, sir?' He glanced round at the *Revelation* study. 'Satan and his followers were fallen angels, remember, but your exhibits depict them as grotesque monstrosities.'

'*Fallen* is the operative word, Professor.' The question appeared to have irritated Batterday and he spoke coldly. 'I don't have to remind you that Lucifer means "Fallen star", and that he was cast from heaven. Isn't it possible that his physical, as well as spiritual beauty vanished with that degradation, and he became very much like one of the creatures you are looking at?'

'The medieval church would have agreed with you.' Henson was inspecting the second engraving once more. 'But this fellow with the club interests me. Can you give him a name?'

'No.' Their host's tone was even colder. 'Is there any reason why I should be able to?'

'Only because he seems to be present elsewhere. In the hunting scene . . . standing at the entrance to the cave . . . also . . .' Henson had spotted a crudely-executed woodcut by the window and he hurried over to it, screening his eyes against the thin autumn sunlight glinting through the glass. 'Yes, surely this is the same personage. A bearded man followed by a flock of birds that could be either geese or swans, and the title is *Die sieben Pfeifer*, which seems to confirm that . . .' He paused, clapped a hand to his forehead and swayed slightly. 'But what a fool I am! What a blind fool.'

'Are you unwell, Professor?' 'What's wrong, Herbert?' Batterday and Tania spoke in unison, because he really did look far from well. His eyes had a feverish glaze and his forehead was beaded with sweat. 'Sit down for a moment.' 'Let me get you a drink.'

'Thank you. I'm perfectly all right, but I've just remembered that I have a most important engagement at the Bedford Institute and it completely slipped my mind.' He pulled out a pocket watch and grimaced. 'Yes, I'm due there in five minutes, so have you a telephone I can use, Mr . . . Mr . . . ?' He stammered and then fell silent as though the name had completely escaped him.

'Of course. The phone's on the hall table.' Batterday opened the door. 'You can't miss it.'

'Thank you. Thank you very much.' The professor walked across the polished parquet floor, planting his feet carefully as if fearing a fall. 'I won't be a moment.'

'Let us hope he will be long enough for us to have a little chat, though, Tania.' Batterday had watched Henson move down the corridor and then he closed the door. 'Now, just how well do you know our friend and exactly what does he want from me?'

'About as well as I know you, John. He's an acquaintance of Mark's; a consultant psychologist at St Bede's.'

'So you said when you rang me.' He crossed to a sideboard and produced glasses and a bottle of sherry. 'But why is he so interested in my affairs? What is he really after?'

'But I told you, John. Henson's interested in art and when I mentioned your collection he wanted to see it.' Tania watched Batterday open the bottle, twisting the cork with strong gloved hands while his eyes stared fixedly at her. Sadness and suspicion and tension flowed from him like a physical odour and she knew she couldn't go on lying. 'Very well, but please don't be angry. Henson is one of the editors of the *Psychic Observer*, a magazine dealing with extra-sensory phenomena. He came across some newspaper reports which mentioned your name and he wants to discuss the events with you.'

'What reports? Which events, Tania?' He poured out the sherry and came towards her with the glasses. 'Why should he want to spy on me?'

'The *Marie Treverith* ... the Liverpool fire ... that wretched business on the moors.' Her answers had lessened his tension slightly, but Batterday was still very much on his guard. 'Is that all that interests him? All that he has heard about me?'

'As far as I know, John.' Tania's own guard came up as he stood frowning at her, because another emotion showed in his face and it disturbed her deeply. This was the first time she had been alone with John Batterday. Mark had always been present at their former meetings, and their relationship was very much a surface one, as she had told Henson. But now she realized that Henson's curiosity was not the only cause of Batterday's tension and she stepped back after taking a glass from him.

A lonely man living in a cheerless, antiseptic house. Sleeping like a monk – she had once glanced into his bedroom and it was as spartan as a cell. Painting pictures for children that were charming, if a trifle sentimental. Collecting pictures that had no charm at all. Batterday had told Mark he'd never been married and she'd imagined he was a cold fish sexually, with no need for women.

But now she saw that she was wrong – quite wrong. He might be disturbed by the professor's visit, but it was she who was disturbing him now and she prayed that Henson would not be long on the phone. John Batterday wanted her – he was craving her body as an alcoholic craves drink, and his frown had changed to open desire. He had put down his glass on the table and his left hand was clutching the cuff of his right glove. She knew that he was fighting the urge to rip it off and reach out for her, and she took another pace back.

'That's taken care of.' The door opened and Henson bustled into the room with a smile. The indisposition, if that was what it was, had passed and he looked as though he had received good news. 'Thanks to your telephone, Mr Batterday, I'm out of trouble and they've postponed my appointment till one o'clock.' He did not hesitate over the name this time, but his smile faded at Batterday's expression.

'But what's the matter, sir? Have I done something to upset you?'

'Not yet, Professor Henson, though I imagine you soon will do so.' There was no lust in Batterday's face now and his tension had lessened. He sounded embarrassed and irritated like a man being asked to lend money to someone he has slight wish to help. 'Tania has told me why you are here.'

'Has she indeed? Tch . . . tch . . . tch. You're a naughty girl, my dear.' Henson was not at all put out and he smiled again while reaching in his pocket for the press cuttings. 'I was hoping to introduce the subject tactfully, but time's getting on, and I'd be grateful if you would be kind enough to answer a few questions in the interests of science. Your name's an uncommon one, and I presume these refer to you, sir.'

'Yes, I am that unlucky man, Professor, and I can guess what your line of questioning can be.' Batterday took the clippings from him and glanced briefly at them. 'When the pleasure launch *Marie Treverith* capsized off the Lizard in 1966 I was the sole survivor and it was three days before an R.A.F. helicopter found me clinging to the wreckage.

'I was also the only survivor of the Liverpool gas explosion five years ago and was buried under the rubble for over forty-eight hours.' He handed the papers back to Henson and shrugged.

'My most recent misadventure, recorded in the newspapers last December, was due to foolhardiness. I and three acquaintances risked a winter trek across the Pennines and were separated by a snowstorm. I managed to locate a farmhouse and survived, but my companions died of exposure.' Batterday raised his hands with a faint smile that had nothing to do with mirth or humour. 'I always survive, Professor Henson. Long ago I was savaged by an Alsatian dog; hence my reason for wearing gloves. The scars they cover are rather unattractive.'

'And painful when you received them I imagine.' Henson had said he was intensely eager to question Batterday, but his curiosity appeared to be on the wane and he was looking towards the engraving of the Calvary scene. 'But hardly as painful as nails, I imagine.'

'No, not as painful as that, but He died, didn't He? His body gave up the ghost and He ascended into heaven. Whereas I . . .' He was standing close to Henson and speaking so quietly that Tania could barely hear him.

'I live on, don't I, and being close to death is not the same thing as dying, as you appear to imagine.' He lifted his glass and took a tiny sip of sherry. 'So, what can I tell you, Professor Henson? That I am accident-prone – that I am lucky – that I suffered extreme pain and distress on each occasion I was in danger? That was certainly the case, but I had no sense of entering another plane of existence . . . no expectations of release. I can describe nothing of interest for your magazine, I'm afraid, but I would like to give you a piece of advice.' He lowered the glass and nodded towards three of the pictures: the mockers of Christ's agony – the pit with its beasts huddled around the fire and the human figure watching them from the entrance – the solitary rider following his hounds. 'Do not risk your sanity, Professor. Do not pry into matters you can never hope to understand, because they might destroy you.'

'But I do understand, Mr Batterday.' Henson sounded brusque, almost rude and he gave the name a guttural note as if driving home the suggestion that it was based on a German original. 'In fact I think we understand each other very well indeed. You can't provide me with the information I expected because death is not ready for you. His scythe has not even scratched your skin and you have never heard the Wild Hunt baying behind you. Indeed, how could you have done so, Mr Batterday?

'However, though I'm sorry not to have obtained any copy from you, it's been a privilege to view your art collection, sir.' Henson pulled out his watch; since Batterday had denied having experienced psychic phenomena during his ordeals, his interest in him seemed to have dwindled to nothing.

'Time's getting on, Tania, and I mustn't miss my appointment again.' He stood staring thoughtfully at the dial of the watch as though a problem had occurred to him, and he made her think of someone who had just made an important decision and is unsure of its wisdom. Thank you for your hospitality, Mr Batterday, and please accept my apologies for reviving unhappy memories.' Once again Tania heard the guttural pronunciation of the name.

'And I know you will forgive me, of course. After all, we are both voyagers along the road to truth, though your path has been rather longer and rougher than mine.' He stared around the walls for the last time, his eyes registering a trace of disgust as they fell on some of the more grotesque pictures, and then he bowed to his host. 'We must be on our way, I'm afraid, but let's say *au revoir* instead of goodbye. I'm quite sure we'll meet again in the near future.'

That should have been that. Batterday led them out of the gallery and through the cold, antiseptic passage to the hall with the little studies of humanized animals relieving the deathly white walls. He opened the front door for them, a gloved hand shaking their hands and features that were replicas of Mark Levin's creasing into a brief smile of farewell. Tania set off down the neat gravel path and in the fresh air and the sunlight his desire for her no longer seemed sinister; in fact she felt rather flattered by it. A feeling that was suddenly replaced by anxiety for her car as she reached the garden gate. An American Ford, old, but heavy and powerful, had pulled quickly away from the kerb and narrowly missed the Ferrari's rear wing before lurching away with a deafening backfire that shattered the peace of the suburban street.

'Come on, Herbert.' The professor had not followed her, he must have been chatting to Batterday, and Tania spoke impatiently. 'If you want to get to Bedford Square by one, we'll have to hurry.

'Do let's get along, Herbert.' She swung round and raised her voice, but Herbert Henson was too preoccupied to answer her and it was not a backfire she had heard. Professor Henson was kneeling on the steps of John Batterday's porch. He was craning over John Batterday's body. He was watching a patch of blood soaking through John Batterday's neat, well-pressed suit that had been bought off the peg and didn't quite fit him at the waist.

Three

'Quite true. "Thou shalt not kill, but need not strive officiously to keep alive." A most praiseworthy maxim.' Sir Marcus Levin fingered the knot of an El Vagabondo Club tie while he addressed his student seminar. Like the rest of his clothes the tie was immaculate and needed no adjustment, but he liked the feel of the glossy 'wild' silk with its crossed alpenstock devices and he was very proud of belonging to the club. Its current membership included a royal duke, three peers, more millionaires than a one-armed man could count on his fingers, and a cabinet minister who had only got in by the skin of his teeth.

'But may I quote another maxim, which do-gooders praise but really means very little: "Any man's death diminishes me." In this day and age the opposite is more valid; much more. "Any man's *birth* diminishes me."' Sir Marcus was rarely at a loss for quotations and few things pleased him more than the sound of his own rich, baritone voice.

'Ladies and gentlemen, we seem to have strayed from our set subject of gastro-intestinal infections, but why not? When you are qualified your job will be to preserve human life and you will soon realize that Mr Wilberforce-Smith's digression is perfectly valid.' He smiled at a Jamaican student in the front row of the class. 'Mankind's reproductive powers and scientifically prolonged old age are more deadly enemies than any bacillus or virus I know of. In fact, Miss Philpotts, overpopulation is the major threat to humanity's continued occupation of this planet.'

His smile moved to a very pregnant girl and widened when he saw her blush.

'And the medical profession is one of the main culprits for this disturbing situation. With the best will in the world we have upset the balance of nature and our species has become over-secure and is flourishing too boisterously. Few illnesses mow us down or thin our ranks nowadays. Penicillin has virtually conquered cholera, malaria, yellow fever and the rest of the endemic diseases; Tetracyclin makes short work of our most formidable scourge, bubonic plague, and when one germ strain becomes resistant to an existing antibiotic, the chemists produce a substitute to kill it.' Mark Levin was in excellent spirits. He liked these informal lectures at St Bede's hospital, and he liked the students, who were a keen, intelligent bunch, one or two as cynical as himself. Also, though it was early November, the sun was shining through the window and, after a series of setbacks, his current research programme at Central Laboratories was beginning to reap results. He had every reason to feel happy and, apart from one nagging worry, life was good.

'But because we have been so successful in fighting disease, we are in danger of breeding ourselves out of existence; though the danger appears trivial now. "A cloud from the sea as small as a man's hand."' Mark quoted sonorously because his personal problem had brought the prophet's warning to mind. There was a cloud in his sky, but only a recent one which would soon blow over. Though Tania had seemed withdrawn and worried for the last few days; ever since she had gone out with that pompous pedant, Herbert Henson, there was no cause for anxiety and she'd soon be herself again. Menstrual troubles might be responsible – boredom – there was no doubt that he'd been neglecting her for his work and they both needed a holiday. Whatever its cause, the cloud would pass and it was a triviality: 'as small as a man's hand'.

'Overbreeding and longevity are serious problems, ladies and gentlemen, so what can be done?' He looked at his watch, noting that the session had six minutes to run. 'Are we to adopt a policy of laissez-faire? Leave things to God and trust that He will act in "His mysterious way some wonder to perform", or take action ourselves? Can any of you suggest a possible remedy? Do you imagine that birth control or euthanasia might halt our gallop towards self-destruction?'

'No, Sir Marcus, because they will not be practised while half the world lies shackled in fear and ignorance ... while superstitious peasants are ruled by priests and witch doctors.' Mr Wilberforce-Smith, a vast and pugnacious Negro, glowered at two turbaned Hindus. 'Let us take India as an example ... let us take Pakistan ...' He started to take both countries in scathing detail till Mark cut him short and nodded to another student.

'What about you, Mr O'Brien? I think you advocated voluntary sterilization just now.'

'Not voluntary, sir.' The harsh Dublin accent rasped with bitterness and Mark knew why. The boy came from a large Catholic family; two of his brothers were priests, a sister was a nun, and he had recently renounced the church. Disownment and exile had been automatic and most probably he would never see his parents again. 'I would compulsorily sterilize every man and woman who has fathered or given birth to two children. Also, all persons suffering from heritable illnesses; physical and mental.'

'I see. But are you going far enough, Mr O'Brien? The Nazis would have approved of your last suggestion, but what about racial undesirables – Jews, Gypsies and so forth?' Mark snapped angrily and then turned to the window to hide his feelings, which he despised intensely. The sarcasm was unjustified, anger was a weakness and the past should be forgotten, because Hitler was dead and suffering was over. He had to strip his mind of old bitterness and concentrate on the future.

'All the same, you have a valid point and stringent measures are needed.' He turned to face the class again and his voice was gentle. 'If the race continues to increase so rapidly your children may be as tightly crammed together as my people were at Belsen-Bergen.' An image of the camp flickered behind his eyes. The wire ... the listless huddled bodies ... the constant moans ... the stench of decay. He forced memory aside and considered a present-day image. The Georgian house he had recently bought on Richmond Hill. Airy, spacious rooms, a servants' flat, two garages, a sweeping view of the Thames. A very nice property indeed and a fitting residence for a knight of the realm and a

Nobel Prizewinner, he thought cynically. Tania had been so proud of the place too when they first moved in, and then quite suddenly, only a few days ago, she seemed to have lost interest, and he couldn't understand why, though it was just after she had gone out with Henson. What happened during that meeting to make Tania so withdrawn and preoccupied? Why couldn't she tell him what was worrying her? He cursed Herbert Henson in his mind and again the quotation occurred to him. 'A cloud . . . as small as a man's hand.'

'Ah, Miss Whitelaw.' A timid, mousy girl in the back row had been trying to attract his attention and he nodded to her. 'You have a solution to the problem?'

'I don't know about a solution, Sir Marcus, but an idea's suddenly struck me, though it's probably quite impractical.' She spoke with a slight stammer and was obviously nervous. 'I was considering . . . just considering whether the authorities might be able to lower . . . the birth rate by a . . . a method the public would have to accept through ignorance. I wonder . . . only wonder if an inhibiting substance could be . . . be ad-added to the water or food supplies.'

'Good grief!' Mark prided himself on being unshockable, but he was amazed to hear the suggestion from such a mild-looking person. 'You advocate the contamination of our drinking water with chemicals that produce impotence or sterility. Yes, that would work all right, Miss Whitelaw. It would work a damn sight too well. Hell's bells, woman, we want to avoid a population explosion, not wipe out the whole human race.'

'As I said, it was only a chance idea, Sir Marcus, and I wasn't thinking about chemicals, but something organic and . . . and selective. A micro-organism that would not affect all the population because some people had experienced it before . . . before puberty, and developed immunity.' Though every eye in the room was turned towards her the girl was gaining confidence and her voice becoming firmer. 'For example, parotitis is known to attack the adult genital systems and I was wondering . . . merely wondering whether . . .'

'You were not wondering at all, Miss Whitelaw.' Mark looked at her with a mixture of horror and deep respect. 'You have clearly given the matter a great deal of thought and please accept my sincere congratulations.

'Ladies and gentlemen, the problem seems to be solved; for some of us, that is.' He consulted his watch again and saw that their time was almost up. 'As you all know, the parotitic virus responsible for mumps is usually thrown off by children, who suffer no lasting ill-effects and develop immunity against further infection. But, should an adult contract the illness, there may be severe damage to the male testicles and the female ovaries. Miss Whitelaw has very cleverly suggested that if a suitably-mutated virus was added to our food and water supplies, humanity will not die of overcrowding. A select élite whose parents were immune to mumps will inhabit the earth in spacious comfort.

'Well, that concludes today's session, but I look forward to the next and thank you for your attention.' Mark moved towards the door and then paused as if a sudden thought had struck him. 'Miss Whitelaw, before I go, I'd like to ask you a personal question. Did you have mumps when you were a child?

'Yes, I thought that must have been the case, and this is why your solution does not appeal to me, my dear.' She had shaken her head and he nodded very slowly. 'You see, I and my wife did not.'

'Good morning, sir . . . A lovely day, Mark . . . Hullo there, Levin . . . How are you, Sir Marcus?' He acknowledged the greetings as he sauntered along the corridors to the reception hall; from a nurse who looked quite overcome by his smile, by a young registrar who was obviously proud to be on first name terms with him, by an orthopaedic surgeon, by a middle-aged lady almoner with a come-hither expression that was not really in keeping with her age and profession. To each of them Mark responded with warmth because he enjoyed popularity, the treasured assurance that women still found him attractive, he liked knowing that every member of the staff regarded him as St Bede's most eminent consultant.

He also liked the hospital itself, though the building was no gem of architecture. A tall red-brick pile in the process of long-overdue restoration. Several wards had been cleared of patients and the contractors were at work. The tang of cement and rubble and damp plaster mingled incongruously with the prevailing smell of antiseptics. St Bede's was a house of pain and last goodbyes to many who entered its grim Edwardian portico, but to others the old place was a shrine dedicated to hope and fresh beginnings. What he and his students had said about over-population was true enough, Mark thought, and doubtless something as drastic as the mild Mary Whitelaw's solution would be needed one day. But the crisis would not happen during his or even their lifetimes, and in any case the fight against disease must go on.

'Good morning to you, Sergeant-Major Harrison.' He grinned at the porter behind the reception desk. 'Unless anyone's left a message for me I'll be on my way.' Mark very much hoped that there would be no messages. He intended to look in at Central Laboratories for an hour or so and then get home early and have it out with Tania. He must know if he was right in believing that something was worrying her.

'I'm afraid there is a call for you, Sir Marcus.' Harrison was a resplendent, uniformed figure with an improbable number of campaign ribbons straining against his barrel chest. 'Dr Singh in the casualty department wants to have a word with you. Sent a nurse across asking me to contact you on the public address system. But as she didn't state that it was a definite emergency I told her that Singh would have to wait till your lecture was over.' The sergeant was a stickler for protocol and he wasn't having a senior consultant jumping to the summons of any Indian house surgeon.

'Casualty? That's rather odd.' Mark frowned. 'I'm a bacteriologist, or supposed to be. Not a surgeon or a physician, and accident cases are hardly my line.'

'I told the nurse that, sir, and she said that something had come up which they couldn't make head nor tail of.' The sergeant's tone suggested that the occurrence was a common one. 'Apparently that poor child who was brought in last night from Fulham has taken a turn for the worse. A nasty business that, Sir Marcus. Probably you heard about it on the eight o'clock news.'

'No, I didn't listen to the radio, but I suppose I'd better go and see what Dr Singh wants. Thanks, Harrison.' Mark moved off, cursing the enforced delay. Casualty meant that the patient was an accident case, so probably her wounds had turned septic and Singh had failed to identify the type of infection. It was just his luck that William Travers, the hospital's virologist, was enjoying a week's leave; almost certainly knocking a golf ball about, which seemed to be the man's main interest in life. But why bother him, he wondered irritably. The organisms responsible for blood poisoning and gangrene were easily isolated. Surely any of the resident physicians would be capable of diagnosing the girl's illness?

'Ah, here you are at last, Sir Marcus. Better late than never, though it's a quarter of an hour since I asked for you.' Dr Nanak Singh had been keeping watch for him and came fluttering down the passage. He was a young man, only recently qualified, and Mark's irritation was increased by both his greeting and his manner, which was arrogant in the extreme.

'As your message only reached me three minutes ago, Doctor, I can hardly be described as late.' He looked coldly at his watch. 'I also have other work to do, so shall we go straight through to your patient?'

'In a moment, sir, but it is better I put you in the picture first.' Mark had started to move to the wards, but the Indian plucked at his sleeve and motioned him towards an office door. 'My patient has had a traumatic shock and she'll be regaining consciousness very shortly. A strange face – a brusque approach might distress her.'

'Dr Singh.' Mark took great pride in his bedside manner and irritability was turning to fury. 'I am not in the habit of distressing our patients with brusque approaches, nor am I accustomed to being . . .

'Oh, you're here, Brian?' He raised his eyebrows as he entered the office and saw the hospital dean, Brian Plunket, seated at a desk. 'Is there a real flap on then?'

'That may be for you to tell us, Mark.' Plunket looked up from a report form, and his expression showed that he was also put out by Singh's summons. 'I'm not really in the picture yet and Dr Singh sent for me when the reception desk very properly said you were engaged.

'It's a pretty unpleasant story though, and as usual every cleaner, porter and general dogsbody in the hospital knows the sordid details by heart while the senior staff remain ignorant.' He looked at the report again. 'The patient's a sixteen-year-old girl named Elsie Kerr. A trainee librarian at the Lampton Square branch, with a respectable middle-class background. Father's an insurance clerk ... mother teaches music. Elsie was admitted here at twelve twenty last night after a policeman found her lying unconscious in the gutter of a Fulham side-street. The ambulance crew thought she'd been knocked down by a car, but our receiving officer's findings were rather more sinister. In the first place the child was naked apart from a pair of shoes and a cotton dress. Her other clothes and a handbag were lying beside her.

'But look for yourself.' He held out a typed report form. 'Not very attractive reading.'

'You can say that again.' Mark frowned at the report, which was phrased as unemotionally as if its author was applying for a passport or driving licence. 'Recent and violent breakage of the hymen ... deep scratches around vulva and entrance to the vagina ... bruises and lacerations on shoulders, back and buttocks, possibly caused by cane or light whip with ferrule tip and diamond pattern lacing ... T-shaped burn on forehead ... concussion due to blow on skull by blunt instrument.

'The bastard, or more probably bastards.' Mark muttered savagely. 'Raped, beaten, branded, flogged.' He'd felt a whip several times in his life, there was a number tattooed on his left arm, and he'd believed that no human depravity could surprise him. But this bare, dispassionate account of what had been done to the girl was sickening. 'Has she been able to describe the man or men who did it?'

'Not so far, Sir Marcus.' He had addressed the dean, but Singh answered. 'When she came out of the original coma the child started to scream for help and tear at her flesh, so Dr Mennon sedated her. The only lucid thing she said was that she'd been given a lift in a car. However, there's a policewoman at the bedside and the sedatives should be wearing off soon.

'Now, as to why I sent for you, gentlemen.' He drew himself up importantly. 'Apart from her injuries, my patient is suffering from an infection which is not responding to orthodox treatment. Her pulse and temperature were normal when I took over from Dr Mennon this morning, but they started to mount steadily soon afterwards and continue to do so, in spite of the half a million units of penicillin I gave her.' He paused and looked Plunket hard in the eyes. 'Before administering the antibiotic I naturally telephoned her own medical adviser to make sure she had no penicillin allergy.

'The last thermometer reading taken twenty minutes ago was a hundred and three, and the causative agent cannot be septicaemia, Sir Marcus, because the skin is moist and there's no sign of approaching rigor.'

'A hundred and three? That's not too alarming for a girl of her age, but I'd better examine her at once.' Mark laid down the report and crossed to the door. 'And don't worry, Dr Singh. My brusque approach will not distress your patient.'

His irritation remained while he hurried towards the ward with Singh and Plunket at his heels, because the Indian's anxieties were probably groundless. Elsie Kerr had been beaten and left lying in the gutter with only a thin dress to screen her from the cold. It had been an extremely cold night too, he remembered. He had worked late at Central Laboratories, almost till midnight, and had regretted not having a coat when he left the building and crossed the car park. With her natural resistance lowered by the attack, the child would have been a sitting target for the current influenza strain that was rampaging around London. A strain that did not respond to penicillin, but was definitely not a killer. Singh should have known that and a few shots of Genomycin or Tetracyclin would soon put his patient off the danger list.

There was no need to tell him where Miss Kerr was: the group stationed outside the private ward pointed that out as effectively as any signpost. An obvious plainclothes policeman, three obvious reporters and a middle-aged couple slumped miserably on a bench; just as obviously the parents. They looked up as the doctors approached and Mark halted and smiled reassuringly.

'Good morning, Mr and Mrs Kerr. My name is Levin . . . Sir Marcus Levin, and everything is going to be all right. Your daughter has been through a terrible experience, but she'll get over it,

I promise you that.' He squeezed the woman's arm lightly and, waving aside the journalists who had edged forward to question him, strode into the room.

Elsie Kerr had been a pretty girl once, but now, with her eyes closed, her face bloated and dark with bruises, and a patch of sticking-plaster running beneath her strikingly blonde hair, there was nothing very attractive about her. There was something reminiscent however, and Mark stifled a gasp as he saw her face.

Because his sister had looked very much like that thirty years ago; beaten and bruised and ravished with her features set in a grimace which would haunt him till his dying day, however hard he tried to forget it. There was one vital difference though. Sara Levinski was dead and the soldier who killed her had neglected to retrieve his equipment. A bayonet handle was protruding from Sara's belly when Mark found her in the ruins.

'Temperature almost a hundred and four, now.' He glanced at a chart on the wall and nodded to the sister in charge. A police-woman sat beside the bed with a shorthand pad at the ready and two nurses were present. Mark suspected that one of them should be off duty and had remained out of compassion or curiosity. 'Still sedated, Sister Fenwick?'

'Yes, but she'll be coming round soon, Sir Marcus. The poor lamb opened her eyes a second or two ago and tried to say something, though we couldn't hear much except a repetition of the word daddy.'

'She called for her father, eh? That's natural enough. Please prepare a Genomycin injection while I take a look at her, Sister: six hundred thousand units.' The policewoman had moved aside and Mark bent over the bed. Singh was probably correct in saying that the mounting temperature had not been caused by blood poisoning. There was no suggestion of muscular contraction and none of the characteristic dryness. The girl's forehead was moist, her body completely relaxed, and she made him think of a sailing ship becalmed on a windless sea. Her inertia was both pathetic and disturbing, and anxiety racked him while he felt for the pulse, his fingers avoiding a slight graze on her wrist. Elsie Kerr's fever was unimportant . . . he would soon isolate the agent responsible and find the means to kill it. That was his job, the reason they had given him his title and his Nobel Prize. He was paid for destroying germs . . . he was a specialist who could restore the patient to physical health, but what about her mind? Had her experience driven out intelligence, was there a void inside the skull? Would he be saving a living corpse stripped of memory and intelligence?

But the truth would be revealed soon enough and he whispered a prayer of thanks that his anxieties were groundless. The sedative was wearing off and Elsie Kerr was regaining consciousness. Her wrist was twisting between his fingers, her head was turning on the pillow, her eyes were opening. Opening hesitantly at first, the lids fluttering and closing again, as if the girl dreaded what she might see, and then suddenly widening. Shooting open like camera shutters till they were staring him full in the face. And, at almost the same instant the lips followed suit and she screamed.

'No . . . no . . . no . . . keep away from me, you devil.' The words were like the cries of a trapped bird and the bruised features contorted with terror. 'Stop him . . . stop Daddy . . . stop Devil Daddy.' She had torn her wrist free and clutched at a nurse for help.

'It's him . . . him . . . he did it to me . . . Daddy . . . Daddy . . . Devil Daddy . . .' Over and over again the name was repeated, louder and louder grew the screams, but Mark could only stand there dazed and motionless till Brian Plunket took his arm and hustled him out of the room.

Four

'Let me think. Sir Marcus. Just let me ponder your question briefly.' Dr Simon Blythe Ph.D. was still said to be a competent enough scientist, but he was an elderly man and his voice wheezed and quavered on the telephone. 'Yes, of course I recall having a few pleasant words with you last night.'

'That is a great relief, Doctor.' Mark's spirits rose and he glanced at Tania and smiled. 'Can you remember the time? It was exactly eleven when we met.'

'I can't say that I do, but I know that we discussed my project in some detail and you were uncommonly civil about the progress I have been making . . . very kind indeed. In fact I was extremely flattered by your interest.' Central Laboratories was used by scientists of several fields and Blythe was a marine biologist studying the possibilities of farming plankton for human consumption. He had buttonholed Mark on a landing and bored him stiff for several minutes.

'Eleven o'clock, you say, Sir Marcus. I would have imagined it was rather earlier than that, but let me try to recap my schedule.' He paused in thought. 'I had an early dinner at Vespari's, a *steak diane* which wasn't quite up to their usual standard, and I got to the lab around eight thirty when my assistant was just leaving.

'I packed myself up shortly before midnight. I remember that distinctly because my wife telephoned and told me to come home and quick about it. Delivered her message in good round terms, I may say.' A dry cackle rattled the receiver. 'Time means very little to me when I'm working, you see, but surely it was about nineish when we ran into each other?'

'A church clock was striking eleven, Doctor.' Mark's elation vanished and the images reappeared. Elsie Kerr cowering away from him while she screamed out her accusations and fears. The faces of Singh and the nurses and the policewoman wide-eyed in astonishment. The dean's hand leading him to the door. 'Though I can't explain on the telephone, Dr Blythe, it's vital that I pinpoint the time. We met outside the lavatories, remember, and a corridor window was open. You must have heard the clock strike.'

'Can't say I did, Sir Marcus. Certainly I was coming out of the house of office, but that signifies nothing. Bladder not at all what it used to be and my visits grow more and more frequent. *Tempus fugit*, eh.' He gave another wheezy cackle. 'Memory and hearing getting shaky too, I'm afraid, and I probably didn't hear the clock. However, if you say the time was eleven, let's accept your word. Sir Marcus. Eleven o'clock it was.'

'My word is not enough, Doctor.' Mark's knuckles were white around the instrument. 'Would you be prepared to get up in a court of law and swear that I was at the laboratories at eleven last night?'

'Swear to it in court? My dear fellow, I just don't understand. What is all this about?' Blythe laughed again before Mark could answer him. 'Aha, Sir Marcus, I think I'm with you now. By court you mean *divorce* court, don't you? Dear me, how deceptive appearances are. I always thought you and your wife were a most devoted couple and you've been having a bit on the side, eh? Poor hubby has to work so late, but he finds time to visit a cosy little love nest on the way home.

'And now the Missus has started to rumble the fun and games and you're in trouble. "Oh what a tangled web we weave when first we practise to deceive." ' The old man's false teeth clicked sympathetically. 'I quite see your predicament. Scandal does a chap in your position a lot of harm, and I'd like to help. Been a gay dog myself in the past, though that was a hell of a long time ago. But, however much the lads should stick together, you can hardly expect me to get up in a witness box and commit perjury, eh?

'Tell you what I will do, though. You ask me round for a drink one evening and see that your missus is present. Then, at some point during the social chat I'll mention that we met in the lab at . . . what time was it you want me to say? My memory's a weak reed as I told you.'

'Eleven o'clock. Dr Blythe, but it's no longer important and I'm sorry to have troubled you. Goodbye for the present.' Mark banged down the telephone and moved to the drinks cupboard where Tania had anticipated his needs and was mixing him a whisky and soda.

'Please try not to worry, darling.' She had stood close beside the phone while he and Blythe talked and had heard most of the conversation. 'Though that doddering old fool is no help, other people whom you didn't notice must have seen you – laboratory assistants, the hall receptionists, the car park attendant.'

'I left by a back exit, Tania, and there's no car park attendant on duty at night. Apart from Blythe I'm sure that no one saw me from the time I reached Central till when I got back here.' He took the glass from her and scowled around their pleasant sitting-room. 'The police know that Elsie Kerr was assaulted between ten fifteen, when she left some friends outside a Chelsea cinema, and a few minutes after midnight when the constable found her in

Fulham.' He knocked back half of the whisky in a gulp. 'During that period I have no alibi at all.'

'Even so, there's no need to worry, Mark.' Tania clutched his hand and laid it against her cheek. 'The child was hysterical and nobody's going to believe what she said, because the explanation's simple. The poor kid had had a shattering experience and been sedated. And when she came round the first face she saw was yours. Surely it was natural for her to imagine she was still with the man who raped her?'

'That's how Brian Plunket tried to reassure me.' Mark finished his drink and stood considering the dean's words. 'Most unfortunate, old boy . . . horribly embarrassing, but not to worry because Elsie was in a state of shock and didn't know what she was saying. When she's herself again she'll soon realize the mistake. Just damned bad luck that you were leaning over the bed when she opened her eyes.'

'However that theory won't wash, Tania.' Though Mark was normally a moderate drinker he refilled the glass with almost neat whisky. 'I wasn't the first person Elsie saw. She recovered consciousness from the blow on her head when they got her to the hospital. Oh, she raved all right and tore at her flesh with her nails; that's why they sedated her. But she wasn't frightened of the ambulance men. She didn't accuse the casualty staff of raping her. On the contrary, she kept crying out to them to protect her from this person named Devil Daddy.

'Yes, that's what she called me, Tania.' Though two hours had passed Mark could still hear those bird-like cries following him out of the ward. 'Stop, Daddy . . . don't let him hurt me again. Daddy . . . Daddy . . . Devil Daddy.' He could still see the faces staring at him in the corridor. The plainclothes policeman, the reporters, the parents – worst of all the parents, though their expressions did not distress him as much as their daughter's screams and accusations that had seemed interminable until a further morphine injection gave Elsie Kerr peace.

'And though the child was in a state of shock, I'm damned sure she was convinced I was the man who raped her. If she doesn't retract her statement . . . if the police don't find the real assailant, we're in dead trouble, darling. And even if Elsie does admit that she might be mistaken . . . without a categorical denial I'll be under suspicion till my dying day.'

'Stop talking dramatic nonsense.' Tania was pretending to be unworried, but she knew that what he had said was true and spoke to reassure herself as much as him. Mark might be generally popular, but he had secret enemies who would revel in his downfall. Men who envied him his success and resented the fact that he had left them standing though they had had ten times his initial advantages. 'Who could possibly picture you as a rapist or a child beater, darling? Hell, we've been married a long time and I can read you like a book. Nobody's going to credit the hackneyed story of a mental blackout changing a normal, well-adjusted man into a monster. What motivation could there be?'

'People will believe anything they want to believe, Tania.' Mark took another pull at his glass, and turned to the window. The year was drifting towards winter, today was November the third, but the weather was warm and the distant hills were bathed in sunlight. '*Dr Jekyll and Mr Hyde* is still on the bestseller list and motivation presents no problem at all. Can't you imagine your friend Henson providing a psychologically valid reason for my "schizophrenic loss of control"?' He imitated the professor's pompous delivery.

' "During the war Levin's sister was raped and murdered by a German soldier and he attempted to erase this traumatic event from his mind. A vain attempt unfortunately. Though driven deep into the subconscious the memory festered into a burning desire for retaliation. A compulsion that became so obsessive that finally the mind's control mechanism, the Super Ego, was powerless to resist its demands. The Jewish sister must be revenged by an Aryan child's suffering and Elsie Kerr was an obvious choice of victim. Probably Levin had noticed her blonde Nordic appearance at some earlier date." Twaddle, but it will satisfy the psychiatry pundits.'

'What do you mean, Mark? What earlier date?' Tania had been concentrating on a possible alibi and missed much of the Henson imitation, but now she looked up at him with a jerk of her head. 'You didn't know the girl, did you?'

'Not to my knowledge. I certainly didn't recognize her, but

the facial bruising could account for that. However, it seems she works at the Lampton Square library which is just round the corner from the hospital. I use the reference room now and then, though so do a lot of St Bede's staff. I've seen the dean and Henson and several others there from time to time.'

'That's bad, darling.' Tania was really frightened now. Mark had been told that Elsie Kerr was a virgin before the attack and that she had said something about having a lift offered her. A sensible, respectable girl would hardly have got into a stranger's car at that time of night, so probably she knew the driver. 'Look, Mark, we'll have to be ruthless about this. You must have an alibi and there's no difficulty about that. You got back here around a quarter to one, but I can swear it was much earlier.'

'Thank you, my sweet.' He leaned round and kissed her on the cheek. 'But I doubt if a jury would take your word and in any case it's out of the question.' He nodded at the servants' quarters which were set at an angle to the main building. 'The MacDoggarts had a light on in their bedroom when I put the car away and I saw Mary draw aside a curtain and peer down at me. She and Jock may think of themselves as loyal Highland retainers, but like old Blythe, they'll hardly commit perjury to save my skin.

'No, we'll just have to sweat it out and pray that the police find the bastard responsible and Elsie makes a proper identification.'

'And there is no doubt that the girl was a virgin before the attack?' Tania spoke sharply. 'None at all?'

'I'm afraid not, and it makes the whole thing more horrible.' Mark nodded grimly, his own worries fading for an instant at the thought of Elsie Kerr's experience, and he missed the urgency in Tania's tone. 'How I'd like to get my hands on that devil.'

'Devil? Yes, she called you that, didn't she, Mark? She kept repeating, "Devil Daddy" over and over again.'

'Quite true, but there's a rational explanation for the name apparently. Plunket recognized it as a quotation from *Wuthering Heights*. A boy refers to a man who corrupts him as Devil Daddy, and the parents said that Elsie is a compulsive reader and the Brontës are her favourite authors. The term must have stuck in her mind so that she used it automatically. Used it appropriately, too. Apart from the sexual assault, she'd been whipped, branded and clubbed, remember.'

'Branded? Yes, you said she had a T-shaped burn on her forehead.' Tania lit a cigarette and the dancing lighter-flame brought other flames to her mind. The fire of the pit with the beasts crouched around it. A "T", a whip that left a criss-cross pattern of cuts and a virgin who thought of her attacker as a diabolical father figure.

'Mark, don't you see what I'm getting at? Doesn't it add up? The *Tau* cross is just a T, but Herbert Henson thinks it was once an important anti-Christian symbol. And the whip could have been a ritual scourge, while the fact that she was a virgin . . .'

'Might imply that she was abducted and forced to participate in some Satanic ritual, perhaps a black mass ceremony.' Mark grinned and shook his head. 'Look, my sweet, I'm prepared to agree that such things take place, but I'm damned sure they're mostly undergraduate fun and games and are not nearly as sinister as the newspapers make out. I also know that Henson's been filling you up with lots of unfounded theories regarding the occult, so do let's forget that line of inquiry. When Plunket first discussed the case with me I imagined that more than one man had been involved, but the plainclothes detective said that they were pretty certain a solitary nut was responsible. And judging from his tone I think he was firmly convinced I was the nut in question.

'But what's the matter? Why are you looking at me like that, Tania?' She was staring into his eyes as though she could see something lodged behind them. 'Oh God, not you as well? You're not starting to believe that I may be guilty? I know I've been working too hard lately . . . that I've been neglecting you . . . that we haven't made love for some time . . . but surely you don't think . . .'

'Of course not and you mustn't even say such things.' She brushed a hand across his mouth, and then stepped back three paces and studied him again. 'I was trying to picture you in other clothes and with a different hair-style, and picture is the operative word. Thinking about a collection of pictures must have made me dream up the black mass idea, and you're probably right in dismissing it. The truth could be so much simpler, Mark; almost obvious.' She was still staring tensely at him, but he saw that her expression was becoming more relaxed. 'Isn't it possible that the girl really did recognize you . . . your features that is? She thought you were . . .'

'John Batterday.' He finished the sentence for her. 'No, that notion crossed my mind, but it's too long a shot, too much of a coincidence. He and I have a distinct physical resemblance, we're both East European Jews, but there must be a hundred men in London with similar features. In any case I just can't imagine John's sadistic. His taste in art may be a bit gruesome, but he's such a mild, gentle fellow. Can you see him attacking a child, darling?'

'For your sake I could make myself imagine anything, Mark, but a chance resemblance isn't my only reason for considering Batterday. Up to a few days ago I also thought he was gentle and mild, and rather sexless, but I was wrong.' She sat down on a sofa and pulled at her cigarette. 'You see, last week Herbert Henson and I visited John and . . .'

'He kept repeating that he was all right . . . that he didn't need any help.' Tania tried to revisualize John Batterday waving Henson aside and staggering to his feet. Though obviously shaken and with a greyish tinge on his cheeks he did not appear to be badly hurt and the patch of blood was not spreading.

'Just a graze and my ribs deflected the bullet.' A gloved finger pointed to a hole in the door frame. 'Yes, the damned thing's lodged in there and I'm all right, I tell you; quite all right.' His stance was erect now and he shook his head when Henson demanded to examine him while Tania phoned for the police and an ambulance.

'You are very kind, professor, but I'm all right, perfectly all right. It's only a flesh wound, and though you're a doctor of medicine I would much prefer to dress it myself. Iodine, lint and a bandage are all that's needed and I have them to hand.' He turned and walked firmly into the bungalow, raising his voice when Tania hurried past him to the telephone. 'No, my dear . . . please . . . please do not ring the police. Please do nothing till I come back and explain.' He had moved into his bedroom and they heard him lock the door behind him.

'Somebody took a shot at John Batterday from a passing car, Tania.' Mark had hardly been able to believe his ears. 'Somebody tried to kill him, and you and Henson have not informed the authorities. You both kept quiet about it . . . you didn't even tell me.'

'No, darling and that's why I've been so miserable and worried lately. I wanted to tell you, but Batterday and Henson both said you'd make me go to the police.'

'Too true, I would have.' Mark was angry and he knocked back the rest of the whisky and rapped the glass down on the window ledge. 'Naturally you should have gone to the police; any sane person would. So just what came over you, Tania?'

'I was stupid, Mark, and so was Herbert Henson, but we couldn't help ourselves. John was so persuasive.' She recalled how Batterday had returned from the bedroom and faced them in the hall. His colour had returned and he had changed his shirt and looked physically recovered. But his aura of sadness had increased till it was almost unbearable and Tania had been close to tears before he finished his appeal.

' "Once I did a very foolish thing, Tania, and you and Professor Henson have seen how I am paying for it." Those were his opening words, Mark, and I'll never forget the way he spoke. It was like hearing a confession obtained by torture.

'Apparently John's art business is run on pretty shady lines, and now and then he buys stolen pictures and sells them to private collectors, who can be relied upon not to talk about the transactions.' While she repeated what Batterday had said Tania's theory grew stronger. The opening words . . . "I did a very foolish thing," had been genuine enough, a cry from the heart; but the rest of the story could have been told by a very good actor.

'Well, some time ago John got into a financial mess and failed to pay his suppliers for a consignment of stolen cameos. They demanded their money and what we witnessed was a final threat to make him settle up.'

'What you witnessed was an attempt at murder, and you and Henson kept quiet about it.' Mark's anger had turned to bewilderment. He knew Tania was impulsive and over-generous but he couldn't understand Henson's behaviour. He was a doctor, he knew that bullet holes often turn septic, so why hadn't he insisted that the injury was properly sterilized and dressed? John Batterday had a good general knowledge of medicine, but he was only a layman. To let him daub iodine on the wound showed unpardonable professional negligence. 'You realize you have become accessories to a serious crime, Tania.'

'But I think that you'd have done the same if you'd been there, darling. John was so persuasive . . . so abject and pathetic. There were tears in his eyes while he asked us not to go to the police and it was like hearing a starving child begging for food.'

'He was also asking to be killed.' In spite of Mark's irritation, his personal problem and the mounting worry that Tania might have landed herself in trouble, he was becoming curious. He'd always suspected that John Batterday was a man with a tragic background, but not that he was a crook. 'The next bullet may be better aimed.'

'No, Mark, because his creditors didn't intend to kill him. The shot was just a warning aimed to graze and show him that he must pay up, and he's going to. John said that if he sells his own collection he'll have just enough to settle the account.'

'Umhn! A pretty drastic warning. And I wonder how much those pictures are worth.' Was it remotely possible that the Callot, the Bosch, the Dürer and all the rest of them were not imitations by contemporaries of the masters, but the real thing, Mark wondered, and then quickly dismissed the notion. Out of idle curiosity he had once checked the subject matter at the British Museum and none of the studies were listed.

'After John said that he would square his debt Herbert seemed to make up his mind.' Mark had spoken almost to himself and Tania continued. ' "I appreciate your problem, Mr Batterday," he said, giving the name a sort of guttural pronunciation as he'd done earlier. "If we inform the authorities, you will receive a prison sentence and your creditors will either have friends inside to deal with you, or be waiting for you when you are released: both unpleasant prospects.

' "Well, Tania my dear," he turned to me with one of his pompous bows, Mark. "Thieves appear to have fallen out, but I really can't see that it is any business of ours and I'm sure you feel the same." '

'So because John Batterday aroused Henson's sympathy and your maternal interests he and his associates go scot free. I just hope he doesn't implicate you when the police finally catch up with him.

'But I still don't understand why the man's criminal activities should connect him with Elsie Kerr.' The telephone started to ring and Mark winced. 'That's most probably old Plunket. He promised to call me as soon as there's any news of the girl and it's nearly three hours since she had the injections. The antibiotic should have brought down her fever and she could be out of the coma by now. Who knows? She may be fully conscious and able to name me by name.' He spoke cynically, but Tania saw that his face was ashen as he lifted the receiver. 'Mark Levin here. Is that you, Brian?'

'This is Miss Percy, Sir Marcus, and I have two messages for you.' He recognized the voice of Plunket's secretary, though she had lost her usual deference. The dean asked me to tell you that he and Dr Singh are quite satisfied about Elsie Kerr's condition; physical condition that is, of course. The pulse is normal and the temperature has dropped to ninety-nine-point-three.

'No, she hasn't made any *further* statements, Sir Marcus.' The woman had obviously heard about the accusations and she stressed the adjective while answering his question. 'When I spoke to Dr Singh a minute ago the child was sleeping quite peacefully.

'My second message is from Detective-Sergeant Wilkins, who is in charge of the investigation. As is to be expected, the police may need to interview you at short notice, sir, and wish to know where you can be contacted if the need arises.' The voice was not deferential at all now and there was a gloat and a sneer in her tone. Mark realized that at least one person had pre-judged him and was revelling in his predicament. 'You'll let us know your movements, then? Thank you, Sir Marcus.'

'Evil-minded old harridan.' He replaced the phone and crossed towards the drinks cupboard, but Tania barred his way.

'No more whisky, Mark, and I haven't finished telling you

about John Batterday, so please sit down and listen.' She pointed to the sofa and he obeyed reluctantly, because he didn't feel like sitting. His body was straining with nervous energy and he felt like screaming aloud . . . like beating his fists against a wall . . . like tearing his flesh as Elsie Kerr had done.

'Herbert Henson and I were dupes, Mark. We knew that we were condoning a felony, but John was just too persuasive. We believed his story about the stolen pictures and decided to give him a chance. We were completely hoodwinked and, though you can't blame Herbert, I should have guessed the real motive behind that shot.' She perched herself on the arm of the sofa. 'And if I had done, you'd be in no trouble at all.'

'Sorry, but I'm not with you, Tania.' Mark shook his head. 'Are you suggesting that it wasn't a criminal associate who fired the shot? If so it was a very dangerous yarn for Batterday to make up and I just don't understand why his activities concern me. He may be a crook, his face may resemble mine, but I still cannot see him as a psychopath who goes round attacking children.'

'But I can.' Tania spoke with absolute conviction. 'I'm a woman and I know what Batterday is. He invented that story about the gang of art thieves because he had to give Herbert and me some explanation. He hoped that he could persuade us to take pity on him and we did. But if he'd told us the truth we'd have had no pity. We'd have rushed to the first police station we could find.

'Consider John Batterday's life, Mark. He's not married, and he's got no girl-friend. I'm sure of that because a woman would have left some feminine touch around his house. Yet he is a man with a strong sexual appetite.'

'Why do you say that?' Mark stared at her in amazement. 'We both agreed that he's a born celibate.'

'We were wrong, darling. I know that as definitely as I know you never laid a finger on Elsie Kerr. Herbert had to make a phone call earlier on and while we were alone John brought me a glass of sherry. As he held it out I saw his expression and I realized what his feelings towards me were.' She paused to try and think of a way to describe it. 'For an instant his face reminded me of those Greek masks depicting emotions and what I saw was a man fighting lust. I was terrified till Herbert came back into the room, Mark. I knew that John was struggling to stop his hands from reaching out and ripping my blouse open.'

'You mean that literally? That he might actually have torn your clothes?' Though the account had disgusted him, Mark felt a flicker of hope. 'I see what you're driving at, Tania. You believe that John has intense physical cravings, but keeps away from women for their own safety? That he is frightened of what he might do to them.'

'I don't just believe it: I'm sure it's true. Where sex is not involved John Batterday is a mild, kindly man, as you said, but his sexual urges are violently sadistic.' She stood up and paced the room in thought. 'Remember how antiseptic his house is, Mark. All that white paint and a bedroom like a cell. Those pictures to remind him that damnation and hellfire may exist. They're all dampers, mechanisms to lower his desires, and I wouldn't be surprised if he wore a hair shirt. Yes, indeed he may and that might be the reason why he refused to let Herbert examine the bullet wound.

'But however hard he fights against them, his urges boil over at times and he goes looking for somebody like Elsie Kerr.' Tania lifted her handbag from a table. 'That might not have been a warning shot I heard, Mark. It could have been an attempt to kill him by some enraged parent, brother or boy-friend who considers the legal penalties for rape inadequate and decided to take the law into his own hands.

'So come on then.' She stood dangling the bag impatiently. 'Let's go and get the truth out of him, because Elsie Kerr wasn't Batterday's only victim. God knows how many other girls your *Doppelgänger* has whipped and raped and branded.'

Five

The day had remained warm and sunny, but bad weather was on the way and the birds were taking refuge. Tania was driving and Mark watched the heralds of storm flying inland. Gulls and gannets and, oddly enough, a flock of wild geese fleeing before the high clouds that had gathered in the east. When those clouds reached London they were bound to bring rain.

But for the time being the sky overhead was clear, a few roses still bloomed in the suburban gardens, and the scent of autumn chrysanthemums contended with petrol and diesel fumes. A fine Saturday afternoon with children's voices ringing shrilly from a playing field, women's dresses gay in the sunlight and industrious heads of households polishing the family car.

Just how should we approach him? Again and again Mark asked himself the question. A tentative opening or a blunt and brutal approach? 'Well, Batterday, exactly where were you between the hours of ten and twelve last night?' In spite of his anxiety Mark grinned and a Thurber cartoon crossed his mind. The trembling witness confronted with a gigantic kangaroo while the prosecutor announced, 'Perhaps this will refresh your memory.'

It was going to be difficult . . . damned difficult, he thought once more. How should two private individuals accuse an acquaintance of a revolting crime when their suspicions are solely based on a chance resemblance and female intuition? When they set out he had been fairly confident that Tania's suspicions were true and agreed that it was better not to telephone Batterday for an appointment, but take a chance that he was at home and call unannounced to surprise him. But now, trundling through this pleasant neighbourhood with the blue sky overhead, Mark's confidence was dwindling.

For once Tania was driving slowly; obviously she shared his preoccupation about the forthcoming interview and he could read the name-plates on the well-kept houses. *Costa Brava*, *Lucerne*, *Napoli*, *Tintagel*, and rather originally, *Queen Elizabeth II*. Names associated with honeymoons and holidays and ocean cruises – happy memories of love-making that had no kinship with Elsie Kerr's bruised torn body. If John Batterday lived in some grim, slum tenement his guilt would have seemed more feasible.

Which was nonsensical. Although slums were breeding-grounds for violence, suburbia produced its quota and maniacs are found in the best-regulated families. But though Mark dismissed the thought, the sight of another car polisher suggested two more practical drawbacks to him. Elsie Kerr had said some-

thing about being offered a lift and Batterday had no transport of
his own. Also he had been shot from a car and that meant that at
least two persons were involved, a driver and a marksman. Mark
could credit the possibility that one man, perhaps with a dislike
of the police, whose child, or wife, or lover had been assaulted
might take the law into his own hands. But he couldn't believe in
several people acting together to revenge their loved one. Ven-
dettas might flourish in Sicily, but they were virtually unknown
to England.

And what about Batterday himself? Tania could be right in
thinking that the man fought a constant battle against strong
sexual urges, but there could be a less sinister motive than sadism.
She had told him what Henson had discovered about Batterday
and why the professor had been eager to meet him. But though
John Batterday denied experiencing any psychic phenomena
during his miraculous escapes from death, the ordeals might
have affected him mentally. Seventeen people had drowned when
the launch capsized – nine were killed by the Liverpool explosion
– his three companions on the Pennine walk had frozen to death.
In each occurrence Batterday had been the sole survivor and it
was hardly surprising that he appeared strained and unhappy.
Perhaps he imagined himself to be a Jonah, bringing bad luck
to others. If so he might practise abstinence for fear of involving
someone he loved in misfortune.

Misfortune? The word made Mark think of a German expression, *Schadenfreude*: joy at another person's distress, and he
recalled the voice of Plunket's secretary when he had rung to
report his movements.

'You are visiting a Mr John Batterday at . . . 34 Honeywell Road
. . . the phone number is . . . Thank you, Sir Marcus, I'll pass the
information to Sergeant Wilkins at once.' Malice and glee were
clear on the line and he could imagine her expression after he
questioned her. 'Elsie Kerr, sir. Yes, of course, that poor child in
Casualty. She was still asleep when I last heard from Dr Singh, but
should be conscious soon. And please God that she'll be able to
identify the brute responsible. I'm sure you'll agree that hanging
is too easy for men like that. If I had my way they'd be castrated
and . . .' Miss Percy would obviously have enjoyed advocating

more juicy torments, but remembering that Mark had not been actually charged with the offence she had rung off with a cold goodbye.

The trouble was that though the woman sickened him he couldn't blame her, and he shared her view that castration might be the only way to deal with violent sexual offenders. No restraint was too severe for men who tortured children and he and Tania might be talking to such a man in the very near future. The car had turned into Honeywell Road and Mark's tension rose like the needle of a pressure gauge. In a few seconds they might strip the veneer from Batterday's face and reveal the mania behind it.

An exciting possibility, but an unlikely one, he thought as Tania drew up before the trim white bungalow and they stepped out. The house and the road and the whole area were so well cared-for; they looked so smugly secure that he just could not associate them with violence. He was on the point of telling Tania that they should get back into the car and drive off, and then he shrugged.

The bungalow had been associated with at least one criminal activity. A shot had been fired . . . Batterday admitted to receiving stolen goods . . . they must talk to him. Mark followed Tania up the path. They were clutching at a straw, but drowning men clutch at anything, and he could be about to drown; there was no question of that. Unless the real culprit was caught . . . unless Elsie Kerr made a categorical statement that she had been mistaken his future was ruined. Even if the police considered there was not enough evidence to obtain a conviction, probing eyes would always follow him and few patients relish his ministrations.

'John must have removed the bullet.' Tania paused on the steps to the porch and he saw that a section of woodwork had recently been puttied and re-painted. 'And the door's slightly ajar, darling, which could be a stroke of luck. If we go in very quietly and startle him with a sudden accusation the shock might just break down his resistance.'

'It's worth a try at least.' Mark pushed back the door and they edged forward, the neatness and the unlived-in atmosphere of the house enveloping them like a cold wind: no trace of fluff on the floor, not a stain on the paintwork, not a speck of dust to be seen. They passed the door of the cheerless bedroom, an open door revealing a functional sitting-room-cum-study with ordered lines of books glinting on stainless steel shelves, a dining-room with a stark, white-oak table laid for a solitary meal. John Batterday might employ no domestic help, but a hospital matron would have complimented him on the state of his house. There was a place for everything ... everything was in its place, and only one thing was out of character. Joining the antiseptic freshness of disinfectant and furniture polish was a stench of decay.

'He's in there.' They were almost up to the picture gallery when Mark stopped, hearing the sound of footsteps and a sharp metallic click. 'I haven't a clue what I'm going to say to him, but keep your fingers crossed.' He flung open the door, took a stride forward and then halted dead in his tracks.

The Levins had hoped to surprise John Batterday, but it was they who received a surprise. On their previous visits the room housing the pictures had been as neat and tidy as the rest of the house, but today it was a shambles, and there was nothing left that could be accurately described as a picture. Broken glass littered the parquet floor, and the canvases and prints that the glass had once screened were mutilated. The study of Christ's agony on the road to Golgotha, which Mark had briefly considered to be a Dürer, had been slashed, the *Seven Whistlers* was daubed with ink or blue paint, the *Wild Hunt*, as Henson had described the engraving, hung in shreds from its frame. Every exhibit had suffered in some way and the big oil painting based on the *Revelation* of the Pit had been treated more meticulously than the others. Each beast had a blackened hole bored through its eyes.

But vandalism was not the only surprise in store for Mark and Tania. They had expected to confront an acquaintance, but the two men stationed beside a desk they had just prised open with a jemmy were quite unknown to them. One was young, almost a boy, with a slim athletic figure, while his companion was middle-aged and sallow and running to fat. But though their physiques differed, their manner was identical. They were bland and jocular, suspicious and domineering, all at the same time.

'Ahaha! Home at last, eh.' The elder of the two smiled pleasantly. 'Sorry about the forced entry, but we've been worried about you, sir. Rather concerned for your well-being.'

'Also a wee bit vexed.' His youthful companion smiled in turn and then nodded at a passport lying on the table. 'Rather annoyed with you, sir, I'm sorry to say.'

'Annoyed, Alfred? That's no way to talk to the gentleman.' The middle-aged man picked up the passport and held it towards Mark. His smile remained, but there was nothing pleasant about it now. 'We're not annoyed, we're bloody furious because we don't like forgers and thieves. We don't like 'em one little bit, Mr Batterday.'

'An extraordinary resemblance. Sir Marcus, and I trust you will forgive our rather discourteous greeting.' The older man handed back Mark's driving licence and credit card, but retained a visiting card. His name was Detective-Inspector Frank Moxton and he had heavy, sagging features and a wart on his left cheek. On the surface he looked rather stupid and ineffectual, but his eyes betrayed him. They were hard and bright, as if pebbles had been screwed into the sockets by some revolting piece of surgery, and very, very shrewd. As he himself liked to remark, 'there weren't many flies on old Frankie Moxton.'

'But it's a cliché to say that passport photographs are not much to go on, isn't it, Lady Levin?' Titles impressed the inspector and he pronounced Tania's with a flourish. He was a snob who liked important people and he thought of himself as a watchdog – a guardian of the establishment with his teeth at the ready for all who threatened it. 'If Constable Steele and I had seen Mr Batterday in the flesh, I'm sure the misunderstanding would never have arisen, would it, Alf?'

'Maybe not, sir, but the likeness is really striking, Inspector.' The young man was studying the passport. 'You're not related to Mr Batterday, I presume, Sir Marcus?'

'No, just an acquaintance. My wife and I share Batterday's interest in art.' Mark stared around the walls trying to imagine the kind of mentality behind the destruction. 'We happened to be passing and thought we'd drop in and pay him a call.'

'Only an acquaintance, you say, sir.' Moxton raised his eyebrows. 'Yet you know Mr Batterday well enough to creep into his house without ringing the bell.'

'The door was ajar, Inspector.' Mark groped for a suitable lie. In other circumstances the sensible course would be to tell Moxton the exact truth, but that was out of the question. By not reporting the shot fired at Batterday, Tania had laid herself open to a serious charge. 'As it happens we thought you were burglars. Inspector. While coming up the path my wife saw one of you bent over the desk and theft seemed obvious.'

'Your courage does you great credit, Sir Marcus.' Moxton's tone made it clear that Mark's intelligence did not. 'So one can say that you were on friendly terms with Mr Batterday.' He grinned at the jemmy on the desk. 'Friendly enough to risk bodily harm in defence of his property.'

'We only saw one of you, Inspector, and felt that it was our duty to investigate.' Tania answered almost automatically and her mind was reeling with questions. Why were the police here – where was Batterday – who had destroyed his collection? Above all what caused that sweet, sickly smell drifting in from the passage? She shivered slightly as a possible solution occurred to her. If Batterday was a psychopath, as she suspected, Elsie Kerr might have been more fortunate than a previous victim. Would Mark be exonerated by a rotting corpse? 'But would you please tell us what's going on?'

'Monkey business, Lady Levin, but not to worry about that pong.' Moxton had read Tania's thoughts and he sniffed ostentatiously. 'That's not a dead body you can smell, but a joint of uncooked beef that's reposing on the kitchen table. Been there for about a week, if I'm any judge of decomposition.'

'A week? Then where is Batterday? What's happened to him?'

'We hoped you might be able to tell us, Sir Marcus.' Constable Steele replied to Mark's question. 'Mr Batterday often goes off for a few days: to auction sales and so forth, and in the past he always left word at the station for us to keep an eye on the house. But this time he didn't ... he didn't cancel his milk either, and when a passing constable noticed that there were three bottles on the step and no curtains drawn he took a look around.' Steele pointed at the window. 'Flashed his torch through there and what he saw made him radio for a patrol car in a hurry.'

'I don't wonder.' Mark studied the ruin of Batterday's pictures and he noticed that they had all been mutilated in different ways: some slashed and torn, some daubed, some burned and perforated. 'While the man's away somebody breaks in and does that to his collection. It must have been a maniac, Inspector.'

'Maybe, sir. There are plenty of those gentry about.' Moxton nodded almost absent-mindedly. 'He would have to be a pretty skilful loony, however. All the doors and windows are fitted with thief-proof catches which were intact till our chaps caught a whiff of bad meat through the letter box and broke in. The joker either had a key or he was damn good at lock picking.

'And apart from destroying the pictures he left no traces of his visit. Nothing seems to be stolen and we've found no fingerprints.' The bright eyes were very thoughtful. 'I just can't understand that. The house is not only as clean as a whistle, there isn't a fingerprint anywhere.'

'Mr Batterday's hands were badly maimed, Inspector, and he always wore gloves to hide them.' Tania heard Moxton thank Mark for the information, she saw Steele enter it in his notebook, but an image of scarred fingers tearing at a girl's body flitted through her mind and she concentrated on her theory. She must be right – she had to be right – and the puzzle was fitting together. It was just a week since the shot had been fired at John Batterday, and he had left home to avoid his would-be murderers. He had hidden away in some hotel or boarding house and, sick with fear and anguish, made a vow that he would never lose control of himself again.

But the vow had not been kept. Desire was too strong for him, and when it became unbearable he had hired or stolen a car and driven around the streets till he found little Elsie Kerr. Tania could visualize everything, but the final scene was the clearest, because she was in the room where it took place. John Batterday had come home and he would have been out of his mind with remorse . . . with self-hatred and disgust. As a penance he had destroyed the pictures he treasured and made off again, perhaps intending to leave the country, maybe to kill himself. But, whatever his intentions, Batterday had to be found, found quickly, and Tania made up her mind. One fact was needed to prove her correct and then she would tell Moxton and Steele everything. 'At what time did the constable come to the house, Inspector?'

'He called the station at eight thirteen last night, Lady Levin.' Moxton answered indifferently, but the reply made Tania stifle a gasp of disappointment. The pictures were damaged long before Elsie Kerr was even abducted and her theory was tottering. Batterday's story must be true after all. He owed money to a gang of thieves and after the warning shot they'd come round to collect. They had picked a lock, crept in to surprise him, as she and Mark had hoped to do, and found that their debtor had fled. Tania looked at the blue daubs on the hunting scene, the slashes across the print of Calvary, the holes burned in the faces of the Beasts. Mindless, brutish anger had prompted the destruction, it had nothing to do with Elsie, and Mark was still in trouble. She turned to the inspector for more confirmation. 'You mentioned thieves and forgers when we came into the room. I suppose you've discovered that Batterday was a receiver and also dealt in stolen pictures.'

'Not so far, but thank you for putting the idea into my mind.' Moxton circled the room and Tania saw that he shared Herbert Henson's distaste for the exhibits. 'Forging old masters, eh: if that's how one would describe these monstrosities. I suppose we'll have to get an expert to examine them.

'Now hand over that passport, Alf, there's a good lad.' He opened it for their inspection. 'This is why I mentioned theft and forgery, Sir Marcus, and it's going to land your friend ... sorry, acquaintance, in serious trouble. Born at Riga, Latvia, in 1925 and granted British citizenship in '46. Since then Mr Batterday has been a bit of a bird of passage ... obtained residence permits in several countries, but never stayed long in any of 'em. Maybe pure wanderlust – more likely he made himself unpopular.

'That's not my direct concern, but this certainly is, and it's why the superintendent put me on the case.' He thumbed back to the first page. 'Riga may be correct. Mr Batterday could have been born in Timbuctoo for all I care, but he's not a naturalized British citizen and as soon as we pick him up he'll be shipped back to his country of origin.

'That's what I meant by forgery, Lady Levin.' His index finger ran across the edge of the photograph. This passport was either bought or stolen from its rightful owner and "mucked abaht a bit", as the music hall song went. A fairish job, which would fool the average customs official, but it didn't take me in for long, did it, Alf?' He grinned at the constable. 'If you look at this embossed stamp here you'll see that it overlaps the mark of an earlier impression that was not ironed out completely.

'However I mustn't give away the tricks of the trade, must I, Sir Marcus, and this is why I showed you the document.' He drew the passport aside but continued to stare at the photograph, still struck by its resemblance to Mark. 'Mr Batterday is a crook, so I want the two of you to put all personal loyalties aside and sit down and tell me every single detail you can remember about him.

'And you get busy with your pen and paper, Alf.' Moxton leaned against a wall and waited for them to begin.

'That's all . . . everything you know?' It had taken Mark and Tania a bare ten minutes to make their statements and the inspector frowned petulantly. 'Poor, lonely Mr Batterday! You and Lady Levin confirmed our findings up to now, Sir Marcus. He seems to have no family, and no close friends at all. A few business contacts; mostly foreigners judging from the correspondence that's been checked so far, but not one personal letter has come to light. The desk might reveal something, but I very much doubt it. All we'll find will be art catalogues, bills, receipts and so on.

'Go and see who that is, Alfred.' The telephone in the hall was ringing and he watched Steele hurry off to answer it. 'Yes, a real Mr Anonymous is pal Batterday. If that's not for me, it'll be just a routine business call: a fellow dealer, the grocer wanting to take an order, the bank manager worried about his overdraft. But I'd lay you a fiver that it is for me – the super wanting a progress report, probably.'

'You'd have lost your fiver, sir.' Steele had returned. 'For you, Sir Marcus: St Bede's Hospital.'

'Thank you. Will you excuse me, gentlemen?' Mark's feet felt like lead weights as he moved down the corridor and he noticed that his request had been ignored and the constable was following. Had the local police heard about Elsie Kerr and her accusations, he wondered. St Bede's was in another area of London, but all professions had their grape-vines. Did Moxton and Steele share Miss Percy's suspicions? If so, those suspicions could be heightened in a moment. The call might well mean that the child was fully conscious and had made a definite statement against him. He reached out for the phone, dreading the sound of the woman's gloating voice and lifted the receiver to his ear.

'That you, Mark?' He was wrong. It was Brian Plunket on the line, and the dean was certainly not gloating. He spoke jerkily and seemed worried in the extreme. 'Thank goodness I've caught you, old chap, because it's imperative that you get over here straight away. Something pretty disturbing has cropped up.'

'*Cropped up?* Let's try to be accurate, Brian. You mean woken up, I presume.' Steele had stationed himself within earshot, ostensibly examining Batterday's hall cupboard, and Mark cupped his hand around the mouthpiece. 'I suppose that poor deranged kid has repeated the suggestion that I raped her and people believe it.' In spite of the constable, Mark's voice became strident and foreign: Israel railing against Aryan intolerance. 'And now you want me to appear in an identity parade, I presume. To pose before her bed and endure more ravings?'

'All I can say is that you're needed here.' There was more than a hint of desperation in Plunket's voice. 'This is urgent, Mark, and an ambulance is on its way to pick you up. You'll make much better time than you would in your own car.'

'And I suppose that the crew will include a couple of mental nurses provided with a strait-jacket in case I turn violent. Why not a Black Maria, Brian? Surely that would be even more in keeping?' He rang off before Plunket could reply and stood listening to the wail of an approaching siren.

Six

There had been no mental nurses and no strait-jacket. The ambulance had its normal crew; two stolid men who claimed to be ignorant of the purpose behind their mission. Their sole instructions were to collect Mark at Batterday's address, return to St Bede's as quickly as possible and deposit him at one of the side entrances.

Orders they had carried out to the letter. Tania had followed in the Ferrari, but though she prided herself on being a fast driver, she was soon outpaced. She last saw the ambulance charging across a red traffic signal with the siren at full blast and there was no sign of it or Mark when she finally drew up outside the hospital.

No policemen were in evidence either, as she feared might have been the case. The porter at the side door had only just come on duty and could tell her nothing except the way to the dean's office and Tania hurried off through the stores department, her shoes clicking sharply on the tiled floors and her anxiety quickening at each yard. Were the ambulance men lying, and had Mark been taken directly to the police station to be charged, perhaps? She dodged round crates and chemical carboys and vast bundles of bedding. She was almost knocked down by a trolley grotesquely laden with artificial limbs and her heart was racing when she reached her destination.

'Lady Levin?' A woman in the outer office eyed her curiously, and Tania fancied there was both hostility and pity in her stare. 'I'm afraid your husband is not here. He and Dr Plunket left a few minutes ago, but I was asked to give you this.'

'Thank you.' Tania recognized Mark's handwriting and she almost snatched the envelope from her hand, her fingers scrabbling to rip it open and her eyes blurring as she read the brief message. 'Darling . . . Forget about the "R" business, or at least try not to worry, as things should be all right. But another problem has materialized and I may be caught up for quite a time. Go home and I'll contact you there as soon as possible. M.'

'Things should be all right.' Tears of relief were streaming down Tania's cheeks and she felt slightly faint and gripped the woman's desk to steady herself.

'What's going on, Miss Percy?' she said, seeing the name displayed on a plastic card. 'Why did the dean want to see my husband so urgently? And does this mean that they've arrested the man who attacked Elsie Kerr?'

'Not to my knowledge, Madam, but I'm afraid the police did not take me into their confidence.' Tania had held out the note and the woman grimaced as if eyeing a slightly unhygienic object. 'Nor do I know the nature of Dr Plunket's business with your husband and I would not be at liberty to discuss it with you if I did.

' "The 'R' business." So Sir Marcus thinks you shouldn't worry about a rape charge. Well, maybe he's right.' Miss Percy hesitated and Tania realized she was fighting a losing battle against duty and the pleasure of announcing important news.

'From a snatch of conversation I overheard it seems possible that the devil who assaulted that girl will have more than rape to answer for.' There was another pause: this time to emphasize the statement and make it really hit home. 'I think the charge could be murder, Lady Levin.'

'Sorry about the cloak and dagger business with the ambulance, old boy, but it seemed necessary for security's sake as well as speed.' Plunket had closed the door firmly when Mark entered his office. 'Since that unfortunate incident this morning the place has been seething with gossip and I thought an ambulance would be an unobtrusive way to get you into the building. We've kicked out the reporters, but one or two are still hanging around the main entrance and I don't want you talking to them. In fact I don't want you to talk to anybody till you've had another look at the patient.'

'The patient? You mean Elsie Kerr, of course, Brian.' Mark flushed angrily. 'You also mean, till *she's* taken a look at *me*, so I presume an identity parade has been laid on.'

'Nothing of the kind, Mark, and please stop worrying about what happened in the ward. The child was raving, and when they come to their senses no sane people will believe you raped her.' Plunket spoke with an empty pipe clenched between his teeth. 'Apart from a few neurotic old maids like my Dora Percy, who pictures a man under her bed every night, who seriously suspects you? I'm sure the police don't and though the witch hunters are flapping their wings today the rumours will be dead as dodos tomorrow.'

'Thank you for saying so, Brian.' Though Mark did not believe the assurances, they were pleasant to hear. 'But if I'm not wanted by the police, why did you send for me?'

'Because you're due for some hard work, old boy. The hospital . . . our hospital could be in trouble; real, bad trouble. Elsie Kerr is on the danger list again. The child is critically ill, and there's a distinct possibility that she caught the infection here.' He removed his pipe and picked up a folder from the desk. 'You remember those rejection-control experiments you and William Travers carried out last year?'

'Naturally, though I try very hard to forget them. Will and I have little to be proud of where rejection control is concerned.' Mark grimaced at the folder, recalling the frustration its contents had caused him. The experiments had been attempts to lower the body's resistance to foreign cell tissue in preparation for major transplants, and they had failed miserably. He and William Travers had produced cultures from the blood plasma of individual animals and groups of bacilli known to attack white corpuscles, the system's main defences against infection. The hope was that if minute quantities of these weakened blood strains were injected into a third animal at regulated intervals, they might be tolerated. The host's own corpuscles and antibodies would cease to resist the mild invaders and be prepared to adopt healthy cells: finally a complete organ; heart, liver, kidney.

The experiments failed because they were over-successful. As Mark and Travers intended, the alien tissue was accepted, but the host's defences became decadent, the metabolism was thrown off balance and the animal died. 'But I don't understand, Brian.' He closed the folder and replaced it on Plunket's desk. 'What have our worthless researches got to do with the Kerr girl?'

'Maybe nothing; at least I hope and pray that there's no connection.' The dean sat down and fiddled with the pipe to steady his nerves. 'As you know, Travers is on leave, but I've been on to Tom Wilder, his assistant, and was told that some of the cultures you used are preserved in the cold store. I want to know exactly what would happen if a small quantity of one was introduced into a human being.'

'A single milligramme would be lethal. I can't be accurate about the symptoms, but they would include glandular distur-

bances, acute anaemia and complete lack of resistance to bacteriological infections.' Mark was bewildered by the question. The
cultures were stored in a refrigerated safe and only half a dozen
people knew of their existence. What Plunket had suggested was
unthinkable. 'Death would occur within twelve to twenty-four
hours depending on the person's age and general condition.'

'Anaemia, eh . . . debility, too . . . also glandular disturbances.'
The dean stood up, nodding his head. 'It all ties together, I'm
sorry to say, so let's get along to the ward, I'll put you in the
picture on the way.'

'If I must.' Though Mark's professional interest and anxieties
were rising he dreaded the thought of visiting Elsie Kerr again.
'But I'll just write a note for my wife and tell her that I'm not in
handcuffs.'

'Do that, old boy, but please be quick about it.' Plunket handed
him a sheet of paper and an envelope and then reached out to
answer the telephone. 'Miss Percy, I told you that I was not to be
disturbed under any circumstances.

'Oh, I see. Yes, put him through at once.' There was a second's
pause and then Mark heard Singh's twittering accents, though he
couldn't make out what he said.

'Please repeat that, Doctor.' Plunket looked at his watch and
his eyebrows came up in a bar. 'But I don't understand you. It's
less than half an hour since I saw the child and such a thing is
impossible.

'No, I'm not doubting your word, Dr Singh, I'm just baffled.'
He listened to the Indian's next statement with an expression
of utter disbelief. 'All right, Singh, there's no need to panic. Sir
Marcus Levin is with me and we'll be along immediately.' He
replaced the telephone and strode to the door of the outer office,
frowning impatiently while Mark finished his note.

'The fellow sounded crazy, Mark. What he told me is just not
credible, but we'd better get cracking.' He flung open the door
and motioned Mark to lead the way. 'It seems likely that Elsie
Kerr's in a near-terminal stage, so give Miss Percy your letter and
come on.'

A few hours ago Singh's patient had been on the mend, but
now she was dying. Mark listened to the dean's resumé while

they hurried towards the casualty wing. The girl who had accused him of rape and torture was on the way out and her symptoms tallied with those produced by a group of experimental cultures preserved in cold store. But there could be no connection, Mark was sure of that. The samples were under lock and key . . . there were poison labels on each container, so how could the stuff have reached the child? Even if a member of the staff had been criminally negligent, contact seemed impossible. If Plunket's suspicions were correct there was only one reasonable explanation. Somebody intended Elsie Kerr to die and she had been deliberately infected.

And if she did die, would he be accused of murder as well as rape? Mark had almost forgotten his own worries, but he was suddenly reminded of them by the cold glances of a group of student nurses. He had access to the cultures and he had taken the girl's pulse. There was a graze on her wrist which a fingernail could easily have opened. Would people say that was how the poison had been administered?

'As you know, Mark, Elsie was re-sedated and given the Genomycin injection at eleven thirty.' He pushed his anxieties aside and concentrated on what Plunket was saying. 'Within an hour and three quarters the infection, whatever it was, appeared to be on the wane, and by two o'clock she was sleeping peacefully and the temperature was almost normal. But Singh, quite rightly, refused a police request to wake her up for questioning and decided that a really long sleep was the best cure for her mental condition. He administered a milder sedative, Dormation, and the room was kept in semi-darkness.

'Like Singh the nurse in attendance thought that Elsie was off the danger list; the breathing was quite even, and the pulse steady at seventy-six.' They had rounded a corner and Mark had to force himself to keep concentrating. The girl's parents were again stationed at the end of the long corridor looking even more forlorn than when he had last seen them.

'But two hours ago the nurse noticed an irregularity in the breathing and found that the pulse rate had fallen to sixty-one. She switched on the light and what she saw made her send for Singh.

'But before you examine her I'd like you to give me an assurance, Mark.' They were approaching the ward and Plunket halted. 'If you suspect that the infection was caused by one of those cultures will you keep the matter quiet till the hospital has had time to hold a private inquiry into the leakage?'

'If you think that's necessary.' Normally Mark's eagerness to get to grips with the case would have made him resent the delay, but his morning visit to the bedside made him welcome it. 'But what made you consider that there has been a leakage? The cultures are killers all right, but why do you connect them with the child's condition?'

'The symptoms and the general progress of her illness; response to the antibiotic followed by revival made me feel that we were up against a very unorthodox germ strain, possibly a mutation.' The dean spoke with his mouth close to Mark's ear. 'Up till now all I had was a nagging suspicion that there had been a leakage from the cold store, but if there's any truth in what Singh told me on the phone, I'm damned sure there has been.'

'Then let's find out.' Mark squared his shoulders, forced his face into an expression of professional confidence, and moved on towards the ward. He was suspected of rape, he might have to face a murder charge, but his troubles were unimportant . . . the way the plainclothes detective looked at him over his newspaper was unimportant. He was a healer – a soldier committed to the defeat of disease, and he had a battle to fight. The patient's life and the destruction of the organism that threatened her were the only important things, and he was going to save her if it was scientifically possible. Plunket and Singh had dreamed up an artificially produced mutation because they were out of their depth. The germ must be a natural species and he was going to identify it. He was Sir Marcus Levin who had once knelt before a throne and felt a sword touch his shoulder. He was paid to destroy germs. He opened the door, stalked purposefully across the room and for the second time that day he bent over the bed.

'But I don't . . . don't . . . don't . . .' Mark's first thought was that the dean had taken him to the wrong room by mistake. The second reaction was that his sight was failing, because what he saw was beyond the bounds of credibility. The third that some senseless practical joke had been played on him.

'I don't ... just don't understand.' He raised his head and glanced around the room, realizing that there was no mistake, nothing was wrong with his sight and no joke had been played. Dr Nanak Singh stood by the window in an attitude of complete dejection, the Sister and the nurses and the policewoman appeared equally stricken and Plunket was at his elbow breathing heavily. The stage and the scenery were the same, the supporting cast wore the same costumes and only one thing was different. The leading lady had changed her makeup.

At approximately eleven fifteen that morning a teenage girl with fluffy blonde hair and a pretty face that was temporarily marred by bruises and a strip of sticking plaster had opened her eyes and screamed out at him in terror and revulsion. Now, with the time approaching five o'clock, Elsie Kerr's eyelids remained tightly closed and it was Mark's eyes that had widened in shock; though he wasn't frightened or repulsed ... not at first. Fear came later, because at the moment there was nothing sinister about his patient's appearance. Handsome would have been a kind way to describe the face on the pillow. It belonged to a grey-haired, middle-aged woman.

Seven

'You haven't mucked-out the cow byre, have you?' 'It's time to start the ploughing, isn't it?' 'They say that idleness is a form of disease, don't they?' Captain the Honourable Arthur Seaton-Osterbury mimicked his wife's hectoring tones while he dragged the heavy trolley up the slope and considered a problem which had intrigued him throughout his married life. Why did the lower orders so often phrase direct statements as questions?

'You shouldn't drink so much, should you?' 'You married me for my money, didn't you?' Both remarks were perfectly true, he admitted to himself, pausing to rest and light a cigarette. The trolley was laden with three bins of pig-swill, and tobacco might deaden his sense of smell. He was a bit of a lush, and he had married Molly for money, but why the hell else should he have married her? He'd been down on his uppers, the wolves were closing in on the sleigh, and though Molly was as plain as a pikestaff, she was a prosperous farmer's widow and the best bolt-hole in sight.

Arthur had always fancied the life of a farmer, too. A gentleman farmer, of course, who raised nothing except his hat, as the saying went, but that ambition had fallen on stony ground. He grinned sourly at the similes and glanced back towards the lights of the village. The pubs would be open now, but a lot of good that did him. His credit rating was nil and there wasn't even the price of a half-pint of beer in his pocket. He was a pauper, an enslaved drudge at the beck and call of a miserly harridan who enjoyed keeping him short.

A snobbish harridan, too. Arthur fingered his grimy old school tie, which was the first thing that had aroused Molly's interest in him, and resumed the imitations. 'I'm the last to deny that Arthur spends too much time in the Crown and Anchor, Mrs Hutchins.' He'd heard the bitch say that to a neighbour only yesterday. 'But nobody can say that he's not an aristocrat, can they? Didn't he go to Eton . . . wasn't he an officer in the Tyneside Light Infantry . . . isn't his father the . . .'

'Bitch! Bitch! Bitch!' Cursing Molly made him feel a little better, but she was right of course, though the term aristocrat should be followed by *manqué* when applied to him. His father was a duke and his brother a marquis, he had been educated at Eton and held a commission in a crack regiment. Notable assets in Molly's eyes and the reasons she had agreed to marry him. But when no relatives or brother officers turned up at their wedding, inquiries had been made and the sorry story revealed.

'Your father disowned you and your brother wants nowt to do with yer, does he? Expelled from Eton for gross indecency and kicked out of the army because you was drunk on parade.' Her naturally harsh accent cut through assumed gentility. 'And you're an undischarged bankrupt with creditors after you. Well, I can't pay a bankrupt standard wages, can I, Arthur, and all you'll get from me is pocket money. Five quid a week, and by gum I'll see yer work for it.' That had been said two years ago and despite the rising cost of tobacco and alcohol his pittance had remained static while Molly's venom increased.

'Sodden again, Arthur, and I suppose the pigs haven't been fed, have they?' Another valid statement. He'd woken up with a hangover and visited the pub to have a quick hair of the dog and then resume work. But there had been congenial company in the bar, one drink had led to another, and after staggering home he'd flopped on the bed and lain half sleeping, half daydreaming till Molly's return from the vicarage tea party aroused him.

Such pleasant dreams too. Arthur savoured the images of the Rolls-Royce hurtling over a cliff . . . the yacht sinking . . . the private aircraft plummeting in flames. Each vehicle had contained his father and brother, and how rosy the future would be if one of the events materialized. He'd have the estate and the title, there'd be money to burn and he'd find a very young, very pretty, very-very-eager-to-please little blonde to help him spend it. Above all, he'd hear no more questioned clichés. 'Drunkards are their own worst enemies, aren't they?' 'Cheats don't prosper, do they?'

But he'd better get on, and much as he loathed Molly, she was right again as usual. The pigs had been left unfed since yesterday, the poor sods must be bloody well starving, and it was going to rain. Arthur looked up at the darkening sky and resumed his journey. He didn't want a soaking, he didn't want another visit from the R.S.P.C.A. inspector and he was sorry for the pigs because he liked animals. He always tried not to neglect the livestock and felt deeply ashamed of himself whenever he did. The trouble was that the paddock was such a long way from the farm and the track too narrow for the Land-Rover. Also, just one or two drinks seemed to affect his memory nowadays.

Yes, he was fond of animals and pigs were fine beasts. His spirits improved as he toiled on. He liked their friendly grins, and the way their hind legs tripped daintily through the mire made him think of girls strutting in mini-skirts and high heels. Sometimes he experienced a twinge of sensuality while watching them, and when they were eating his feelings became even more exciting. Great jostling bodies, and powerful overshot muzzles champing away at the troughs. Pigs were omnivorous, they ate anything, and when hungry they didn't leave a morsel behind. They had razor-sharp teeth and massive jaws that could crunch through the hardest bone. Another attractive image crossed Arthur's mind and he smiled. A few of those massive jaws would make short work of Molly's skinny carcass.

'Blast the weather.' The rain had started, a drop of water had extinguished his cigarette, but the slope was easier and his destination was in view. A railed paddock, so trampled and rooted clear of vegetation that it resembled a patch of roughly laid asphalt. Its occupants were clustered together in a far corner and beyond the fence he could see a number of geese flapping their wings and honking at them. Not his geese; not Molly's he should say, of course, because he was a bankrupt who was allowed to own nothing. They must have strayed over from some neighbouring farm.

'Here I am, boys and girls. Grub's up at last.' He shouted loudly, but the animals paid no attention. The racket the geese were making must have drowned his words, but it was strange that they hadn't caught a whiff of the swill. Normally the herd swung round in unison when he breasted the slope and came hurrying towards him like a cavalry squad at the trot.

'Grub's up, I said, so come and get it. Goliath . . . Uncle Tom . . . Lady Chatterley . . . Harold Wilson, what's the matter with you?' Though he bellowed the individual names, there was still no response and overhead a long rumble joined the birds' clamour. When the thunder stopped the rain came in earnest. Cold soaking rain that fell straight down from the almost windless sky and bounced off the ground as if a forest of steel spikes was standing upright.

With his hat pulled low, and half blinded by water, Arthur stumbled on towards the paddock, the trolley wheels lurching over ruts and the bins clattering. 'Hard work never hurt anyone,' had been Molly's response after he asked for a cart with a motor and he cursed her parsimony as he reached the fence and halted. Lightning flashed brightly while he unchained the gate and the second peal of thunder reminded him of a distant artillery barrage. He prepared to unload the bins and saw that the pigs had been frightened by the storm. They were not trotting eagerly towards him, but edging away from some object lying on the ground. Their manner seemed nervous; almost furtive, like children detected at some major misdeed.

'Over here, you stupid bastards,' he shouted, gripping the handles of the first bin to drag it off the trolley. 'Come and get . . .' His shouts faded to a whisper because a flash of lightning lit up the paddock and he saw why the animals ignored him.

'Christ,' he said, stepping sideways to get a better view, but still clutching the handles of the container. 'Jesus unprintable Christ!' The bin tilted forward, reeking swill flowed like lava over his shirt and his jacket and his old Etonian tie, but Arthur Seaton-Osterbury was past noticing smells. His mind was riveted on the thing lying beside the far railings. A hideous and obscene thing, but to his fertile imagination it seemed to suggest that one pleasant daydream might have come true.

'That's taken care of, Sir Marcus.' Nanak Singh lowered a house telephone. 'The ambulance crew, the constable who found Elsie, and every member of the staff who had contact with her have received Genomycin injections now.'

'Thank you, Doctor.' A room adjoining the patient's had been put at their disposal and Mark was studying a report from the analyst which had just been delivered. The data described tests carried out, blood samples, skin and nail parings, sweat, saliva and urine. The chemist had been very thorough and very quick, but he had only provided one useful piece of information.

'The contacts had better have booster shots in six hours time, as well. I don't believe the child was contagious during the early stages of her illness, but we can't take any chances.' Child, indeed! What an unfortunate choice of word. Mark glanced bitterly at the partition dividing the two rooms. The human being beyond that wall had been born less than seventeen years ago, but she was no more a child than he was.

'The blood and saliva tests suggest that Genomycin did check the actual infection but was administered too late.' He looked at Singh, who appeared desperately unhappy and had a pale tinge in his coppery skin. 'Please don't take that as a criticism, Doctor. I was even more deceived by Elsie's symptoms. I thought she had influenza and it was by pure chance that I prescribed that particular antibiotic.

'However, it seems clear enough what happened. Before the drug took effect the glandular system was thrown off balance . . . the pituitary body lost control of his subordinates.' Mark turned a page of the report and recalled his student days and the drone of an old, bored voice repeating a lecture it had probably delivered a hundred times. 'The endocrine glands may be compared to an orchestra led by the pituitary gland, gentlemen. Providing they play in harmony, the concert is a great success. But if the leader goes off key, havoc is created and here are some of the results.' A slide projector had been switched on and examples of cretinism, giantism, mongolism and other forms of glandular deformity glowed on the wall. As he considered the illustrations, John Batterday's mutilated art collection crept into Mark's thoughts. Had Hieronymus Bosch and Dürer relied entirely on the imagination to produce their monstrosities, or had living models sometimes been employed?

'Damage to the endocrine system?' Brian Plunket stood by the window, as if studying the evening sky, but Mark knew that a single image occupied his mind. The dean had been as shocked as he was by the change in Elsie Kerr's condition and he slurred his words like a man in drink. 'Those experimental cultures, Mark? One of their effects was glandular disturbance.'

'Quite true, Brian, but unless we've got a murderer on the premises, I think we can forget that line of inquiry.' Mark turned another page. There was a possible chance that he himself might be named as that murderer, but he was too concerned with the case to bother about that now. 'Dr Singh, when you last visited the patient did you consider her deterioration was slowing down?'

'On the contrary, it was becoming more rapid.' Singh had a little tic trembling under his left eye. 'But what is the infection? What virus or bacillus could produce such changes in so short a time? You must have some idea, sir?'

'I'm not a miracle worker, Dr Singh. I can't see through living tissue with the naked eye, nor am I allowed to commit murder in the interests of science and public health.' Mark had finished the report and he laid it aside and stood up, feeling waves of self-disgust. He had failed, he had no diagnosis to produce and defeat was inevitable. 'All I do know is that the endocrine glands have run amok and our patient is dying. And as that is the kindest thing that can happen to her, let us hope that she will die as soon as possible.'

'Don't be so bloody callous, Mark.' Then dean growled at him without turning his head from the window. 'I appreciate your feelings, but there is no need to talk unethically.'

'Do you also appreciate that my hands are tied, Brian? Nothing can be done to save Miss Kerr and no sane person would wish to save her if he could. But I cannot begin to isolate the creature which has destroyed her till I have the chance to examine specimens of glandular tissue taken from her dead body.' He scowled impatiently at his watch. 'When Dr Singh told me that her condition was deteriorating more rapidly I felt nothing but relief, and so should you. The one thing we have to dread is that her illness may reach a state of passivity and allow her to live for a considerable period.'

'I realize that, Mark.' At long last Plunket turned and faced him. 'But however sick Miss Kerr may be, she is still a patient of this hospital and not a guinea pig.'

'She could also be a source of infection and a hellish danger to others.' Mark prepared to flare back, but swung round because the door had opened and a nurse was beckoning to them. 'Is the terminal stage approaching?

'Then come on, gentlemen.' The girl had nodded and Mark led the way out with the two men at his heels. He walked quickly into the next room, but halted as he saw what lay on the bed; Singh and Plunket did the same, the Indian raising his hands to his forehead and Plunket making the sign of the cross. Elsie Kerr had become a child again. Like old Timothy Forsyte she had grown younger and younger till she was too young to live and her body hardly raised a bulge under the sheets. Her face was hidden by a mirror held over the mouth and when the Sister raised it for their inspection Mark saw that there was no moisture on the glass.

'She's gone, Sister Fenwick?'

'Yes, she's dead, Sir Marcus. A very peaceful end.'

'Does that surprise you?' Mark spoke curtly because he disapproved of sentimentality and he had been longing to hear the news. The shackles were released at last, he could get to work. He could start his investigations and bring a monster out into the open. Soon he would find the means to kill the thing that had destroyed his patient.

Those were his only thoughts as he walked on again, but when he reached the bed his eagerness vanished and what replaced it was compassion and sorrow and fear. Elsie Kerr's skin was wrinkled and as fine as tissue paper; he could see the bones and veins behind it. Her sightless eyes were set in red-rimmed sockets and her thin lips were drawn back to reveal brown, decaying teeth. Apart from a few strands of white hair her skull was bald.

'I'm glad you had a peaceful end, my dear,' he said, very gently pulling down the sheet to reveal the rest of the poor, wasted body. 'But that was to be expected, Elsie. Death is a welcome suitor when ladies are over ninety years old.'

Eight

'We have consumed the flesh – we have released the spirit. He plucked the flower we offered – His journey is over.' Canon Hamilton was rather proud of his delivery and his appearance. He wore lavishly embroidered vestments and the words of the ceremony, which he had personally composed, boomed grandly around the chapel.

'We drank the hunter's wine – We freed the voyager. His night has fallen – Our day is unending.' Hamilton stood on a raised dais before his congregation. The millionaire, the photographer and the mechanic were among those stationed in the front row. Behind them he could see the doctor and the manservant, and further back the candlelight showed up the housewife's thick lipstick like a bleeding wound. With the exception of the old lady in the wheelchair they were all on their knees.

'The doorkeeper is at rest – The child lives on. We have obeyed His will – We shall celebrate His glory.' The canon paused impressively, raised an arm and stepped down from the rostrum.

'*Introibo ad altare Dei.* I shall go to the altar of God.' He intoned the Latin while he moved forward to celebrate the mass; a fine, important-looking man who had been ordained into the Holy Roman and Apostolic Church and held the title of Monsignor.

But there was something wrong about him. There was something wrong with the church and the congregation and the whole order of service. There was something wrong with the altar and the six tall candles guttering upon it. Everything was wrong in some way. The candles were made of black wax and the crucifix between them had no headpiece. The censers that clanked at the priest's approach gave off an odour of sulphur as well as incense. The chalice and patten his servers held out to him did not contain bread and wine; the body and blood of Christ; actual and symbolic. Only the words of the service were correct.

'*Hoc est enim corpus Meum.*' Canon Hamilton raised to his lips a cup of human urine.

'Forget about the "R" business . . . another problem has materialized . . . not to worry . . . go home.' Mark's words of comfort and then five other words designed to wound and frighten. 'The charge could be murder.' Tania frowned at the clock ticking busily away on the mantelshelf and then at the telephone. Almost two a.m.: a foul, wet night with flurries of rain beating on the windows and still no sign of Mark. Still no word from the hospital, though the phone had been kept busy since she had reached the house.

'Please hold the line, Madam, and I'll see if Professor Henson is available.' Tania had made the first call herself and a woman had answered. Judging by the background noises there seemed to be some kind of gathering assembled at Henson's house and she could hear snatches of conversation and laughter. She had had to wait for a couple of minutes and then a door had slammed, cutting off the sounds, and Henson spoke to her.

'My dear . . . dear Tania. I can't tell you how stunned I am by that wretched affair about Mark.' It was clear that bad news had travelled fast and the professor knew about Elsie Kerr's accusations. 'But I'm sure there's no need to worry: positive, in fact. Nobody could believe such absurdities, and if Mark had been arrested you'd have been informed by now. My advice is that you take a tranquillizer and relax.'

'Relax, when my husband is suspected of criminal assault, Herbert?' Tania flushed angrily, though Henson was right, of course. If Mark had been arrested the police or his solicitor would surely have told her.

'Yes, my dear, because if one wasn't so sorry for the child this would almost be a laughing matter.' Herbert Henson might have been soothing one of his psychiatric patients. 'It's quite absurd to think of Mark raping anybody ... completely out of character. Sexual offenders invariably belong to two distinct groups, you see. They are men of low intelligence or suffer from a deep sense of inadequacy. I should hardly place Mark in either of those categories, and when I said relax, I meant it. The guilty party will be picked up soon enough and there really is no cause for anxiety.'

Again he was right, Tania supposed. Who could seriously suspect Mark on the evidence available? What magistrate would sign a warrant, on the strength of a distressed child's ravings?

And yet ... yet ... yet. However much she resisted it, the little word of doubt kept rapping at her ears. Mark himself considered people would prejudge him and Miss Percy clearly did, though after making that remark about murder she had refused to say any more.

And just what had the woman meant by the allegation? Was it a lie invented to hurt on the spur of the moment, or was Elsie Kerr seriously ill? If that was the case ... if she died without retracting her allegations Mark would be in serious trouble. And what if she lived and repeated them? He had no alibi, no witnesses to testify for him, he had no defence except his character, and her own hopes of exonerating him appeared to have been proved untenable. All the same her suspicions about John Batterday had been so strong before the police mentioned the time factor, and she wanted Henson's opinion.

'Umph – Batterday – John Batterday.' The professor had listened in silence while Tania outlined her case and the silence continued for some seconds after she finished. 'Yes, my dear, I take your point. The physical resemblance is uncanny, and that art collection suggests mental derangement. To keep a pictorial torture chamber devoted to hell and damnation is about as morbid as you can get. And if his guilt complex is really obsessive he probably imagines that three agonizing escapes from death were divinely inspired punishments or warnings.

'So far, so good, Tania, and you're right in saying that men who repress strong sexual urges can become very dangerous customers. But while agreeing to your general thesis I just can't see Batterday as a sadist. He's such a pathetic, shadowy sort of character: more the masochistic type to my mind.' Henson's soothing tone became a little brusquer. 'But please tell me what the police had to say about his disappearance in more detail.

'Then there we are, Tania.' He had listened in silence again and there was no comfort in his tone when he resumed. 'The milk bottles show that Batterday made himself scarce several days ago and the pictures were destroyed before the girl's abduction. That rules him out, doesn't it? The man's story was true. Our friend Batterday is just a cheap crook, so do let's forget him and remember our joint promise to say nothing about the shooting. The police would take a very poor view of us for keeping silent.'

'To hell with us, Herbert.' Tania flushed a second time. 'My husband is suspected of rape; possibly murder as well.'

'Murder? What on earth do you mean? I understood the girl was in no physical danger.

'Oh, the dean's secretary told you.' Henson sounded immensely relieved by her answer. 'Then most likely there's nothing to it. In my opinion Dora Percy has paranoid tendencies and she'd lie her head off for the pleasure of making you squirm.

'All the same, if there is any truth in what she said . . . if the Kerr girl is on the danger list, things could be serious. Supposing she died without admitting she was mistaken about Mark and the true rapist is never brought to book . . . Yes, that would be extremely serious.' Henson's tone showed deep and genuine anxiety and Tania's annoyance faded. 'Look, my dear, I'm going to ring off and get through to the hospital. If there's any truth in Dora Percy's implication and the child is really ill, I'll call you back. But I'm almost certain the bitch was lying and you've no cause to worry.'

Henson had not rung back, but that did not prove Miss Percy a liar. Tania's phone had been constantly engaged and when she got through to the hospital herself the receptionist was strangely reticent. No private calls could be accepted by the casualty department, nobody was available at the dean's office, there was no information regarding Mark. Her husband's whereabouts remained a mystery, though a great many people had heard the accusations against him. Tania looked at the telephone with a mixture of dread and hope. The number was ex-directory, but they had a large circle of friends and acquaintances and even after midnight the condolences had kept flooding in.

'Tania, darling, my thoughts are so much with you.' One caller had been a woman with whom she sometimes played golf. 'I wouldn't have believed it, if Nancy Keating hadn't told me herself; her son's a student at St Bede's, you know. I felt I had to ring and offer my sympathy. Peter and I always thought your marriage was such a happy one and . . .'

'Lady Levin, I am stunned by your news.' Tania had hung up on her golfing friend but the next call followed immediately and the voice of the Reverend James Raven, the local vicar, wheezed from a public phone booth. 'One of my flock who is a cleaner at the hospital just told me, and I would like to offer my most sincere sympathy in your time of trial. Also, some advice which I hope you will not think presumptuous. Do not condemn your husband too harshly, dear lady. Whatever Sir Marcus has done . . . however great his sin, he is not personally to blame. Satan is always lurking in the shadows to ravage and destroy and lead one into temptation, so remember the prayer, "Forgive us our trespasses," and show mercy.'

'Called to see if I can help, Tania.' The voice had belonged to Fat John Forest of the *Daily Globe*. 'The press can be a good friend, if it wants, and I believe a story from you might clear the air. Naturally I've not the slightest doubt about Mark's innocence, but the public love seeing an eminent man involved in anything unsavoury, and we must pander to their gruesome little minds.' A chair creaked as Forest eased his vast bulk into a more comfortable position. 'But a frank article from you should work wonders, and by frank, Tania, I mean sordid. Make out that your sexual relations with Mark are too active for him to have the energy to chase teenage girls. Or, better still, we might invent a mistress or two as curbs for his ardour.'

To hell with them! Mark had told her not to worry, but how could she help worrying with so many well-wishers who clearly believed in his guilt! Even their own staff had given her no comfort. When she had confided in the MacDoggarts, Mary had looked incredulous while Jock had thumped the kitchen table and announced that 'Naebody but a loon would credit sich a diabolical accusation against the maester.' But when Tania had probed their loyalty by saying there was no need to worry because Mark had been home at ten thirty, Jock's face had become embarrassed and Mary had stared silently at the floor.

Why couldn't Mark call her? Why on earth didn't the police or somebody at the hospital tell her what was going on? Tania went to a window and pulled back the curtains. The rain was lessening, but a strong wind had blown up and the trees were bowed before its gusts. The straining branches made her think of witches riding their broomsticks through the night sky and once more she considered John Batterday and his bizarre art collection. The suggestion was that the pictures had been mutilated by criminal associates, but surely something stronger than an unpaid debt must have motivated such insane destruction? To rip and slash at paintings – to daub them with ink – to burn holes in canvases and tear prints from their frames hinted at rage over some deep personal injury. The kind of emotion she might have felt if a child of her own had suffered as Elsie Kerr had done.

Tania tried to reconsider her theory dispassionately, but she soon gave up. She was too tired, too disturbed and wretched to think clearly and she couldn't stay in the house any longer. Mark had promised to contact her at home, his note implied that he was less worried about the girl's accusations, but it was eight hours since the ambulance had carried him off. She couldn't stand any more waiting, she'd go to St Bede's, and if necessary she'd scream the place down till they told her exactly what was happening.

Tania picked up her bag, walked quickly over to the door and then stopped with her hand on the knob. The phone was ringing again and she felt half inclined to leave without answering it. The caller might have news of Mark, it might even be Mark himself, but most probably she would hear the voice of another inquisitive sympathizer, and she couldn't take any more of them. For a full fifteen seconds she stood hesitating and then lifted the instrument.

'Could I speak to Sir Marcus Levin please?' The man sounded vaguely familiar, but she couldn't place him at first.

'Oh, good morning, madam.' She had replied that Mark was not at home and he introduced himself. 'This is Detective-Constable Steele of Brantwood Road police station, and we met this afternoon at the house of Mr John Batterday. I do apologize for disturbing you at such an hour, but Inspector Moxton hoped that Sir Marcus might be prepared to help us. You see, we may have located Mr Batterday, but need an identification.'

'You've found him . . . you've found John Batterday.' Tania's face was radiant. Batterday must be using an alias, but he was under arrest and her worries were over. Very soon Moxton and Steele would break him down and hear a confession of rape and torture. 'Constable, I've no idea when my husband will be back, but can't I help you? I know Batterday quite as well as he does.'

'I'd be very grateful if you would, madam. We're out in Surrey, a place called Asterford, but I can radio a squad car to pick you up in a few minutes, if that's convenient. However, I must warn you that you'll be in for a bit of an ordeal.'

'That won't bother me, Mr Steele. I'll be ready when the car arrives, but please give me a few details before you ring off. Obviously the man's claiming to be someone else, but what is he charged with . . . where was he arrested?'

'Arrested?' The policeman gulped and then became apologetic. 'I'm so sorry, Lady Levin, but I haven't made myself clear. What we want you to look at is a dead body.'

Nine

'Missouri . . . She's a mighty water . . .' Mark hummed the shanty while he waited for his assistant, Paul Johnston, to fit a slide into the hospital's big electron microscope. 'The Indian camp lies on her quarter . . . Away, I'm bound a-way . . . Cross the wide Missouri.' Johnston had stepped aside and Mark took his position at the eyepiece and adjusted the focus. This was the sixth specimen he had examined and he knew what he would see: debris, the litter of a battlefield that humanity had lost because its armies had been unprepared for the alien invasion.

'The Indian camp lies on her quarter ...' He repeated the line because it seemed appropriate to what he was looking at. Along the left hand corner of the slide ran a blur – a dark shadowy zigzag which he suspected was a camp of the enemy.

'Oh, Shenandoah, I love your daughter ... For seven long years I have not seen her ...' He twirled the fine control knob and suspicion hardened into near certainty. The evidence of cell wastage was unmistakable. Mr and Mrs Kerr's daughter was dead but it had taken more than any seven years to kill her. Elsie had died because she was too old to go on living, and towards the end the ageing process had accelerated with each heartbeat. Just before that tired heart had fluttered to a halt, she had been growing old at the rate of two months for each minute of actual time.

'A-way, I'm bound to go ... Cross the wide Mis-sou-ri.' Mark straightened from the instrument, having seen all the specimen could tell him. Their patient had been taken across the river, and he knew the reason for her journey. What had he to do now was to name the ferryman.

'I think you can stop worrying about a theft or accidental leakage from the cold store, Brian. The only cultures Travers and I preserved were bacteriological mutations and there's no suggestion that a bacillus was responsible. As I thought earlier, it's pretty clear that the orchestra leader killed her.' He smiled grimly at Plunket and Singh. 'The pituitary gland went haywire, his fellow musicians followed suit and with the whole endocrine system at loggerheads, senility was automatic.

'No, Dr Singh, I've still no idea what triggered off the situation, though there are certain indications that the agent may have been fungoid.' He watched Paul Johnston preparing another slide. 'That's just guesswork at the moment, but the nature ... the course of the illness is definite enough. Her condition was similar to Progeria, though much more rapid.

'Precocious Old Age is another name for it, Brian.' The Indian's face was eager, but the dean's remained blank. 'Progeria's a mercifully rare complaint; about one person in a million suffers from it and the majority die in infancy. I've never seen a case myself, but I think there was one reported not so long ago.'

'There was indeed, Sir Marcus. It occurred in South America, and I read a most fascinating article on its history.' Singh was pleased to air his knowledge. 'The victim was a boy of twelve named Jomar Henrique Silva, who had suffered from Progeria since birth, and died while playing with his toys. Coronary failure – Stokes-Adams disease – senile degeneration of the heart was the actual cause of death, but this is the interesting thing; Jomar had the mind of a child, but his body belonged to a very old man. White hair, wrinkled skin, hardened arteries. In fact, what we saw recently, gentlemen.'

'Progeria. Yes, I'm with you now.' Plunket nodded. 'But as you say, that's a mercifully rare complaint, Mark, and I don't think I've heard it mentioned since I was a student. And surely Progeria is not caused by infection? It's an inborn glandular malformation and the ageing process is only increased about six-fold. The boy Dr Singh read about was born with the malady, and he lived to be twelve. Whereas our patient . . .' The dean spoke slowly to gather his thoughts and his eyes, like Mark's, were fixed on the laboratory bench where Johnston's scalpel was slicing through a morsel of reddish tissue about the size and shape of a pea: *Hypophysis Cerebri* – the pituitary body. One of the supreme governors of human destiny which had turned into a rogue. 'Elsie Kerr's own doctor reported that she had no congenital illness and was a perfectly healthy child. Then suddenly . . . in a matter of hours . . .'

'She became a crone of about ninety.' Plunket had broken off with a shake of his head, and Mark resumed. 'I did not mean to imply that she suffered from actual Progeria, gentlemen. Only that her glandular disturbance produced the same symptoms.' He considered what he had seen in the ward. The shrunken body with its bones staring through wrinkled transparent skin, the shreds of white hair, the decayed teeth and the red-rimmed eyes. He was a scientist, he had always been quite dispassionate towards the tiny enemies he fought to destroy, but he suddenly felt a wave of personal hatred towards the thing that had ravaged Elsie Kerr.

'What is it, Paul?' The next slide was in position and he heard

Johnston give a whistle of astonishment as he looked through the second eyepiece. 'Have you something definite at last?'

'I think so, sir. In fact I'm damn sure we have. Look for yourself.'

'You're right . . . you really are right.' Mark was already bent over the microscope and what he saw brought sweat prickling on his forehead. The image was as clear as a photograph and it told him that his first suppositions were correct.

'The invaders had died quickly. Antibiotics injected into the bloodstream had wiped them out, but serious pituitary damage had been done before that battle took place and the war had continued. The hostile camp was no vague blur on this specimen. It stretched right across the picture and he could see craters and fissures and hillocks. The rubbish dumps of defeated armies that had left their garbage behind. Dead cells and other waste products to irritate the already damaged gland till it went berserk and its partners followed suit. The endocrine system had become a wolf pack to ravage the body it was designed to defend.

'The hormones would have been thrown off balance too, Paul, and we've got a real monster to deal with.' Mark studied a line of tiny star-shaped dots. 'A little horror that's like nothing I've seen or read about.

'No, I could be wrong. The units do remind me of something and I'm pretty certain they're fungoid. A genus rather similar to the *Streptothra madura* group.'

The organism responsible for Madura Foot?' The dean was at his elbow. 'But that's a tropical illness, Mark. To the best of my knowledge we've never had a case at St Bede's, so when and where could she have picked up anything of that nature?'

'Last night during the hours the child was missing and somewhere in London or the Home Counties, I imagine. But the important question is *from whom?*' Mark knew more or less what he was up against now. He also knew what might be about to happen in the very near future and his whole face was damp with sweat as he drew back from the microscope.

'Mr Dean,' he said formally, 'you have suppressed the details of this case to all unauthorized persons and you asked me to make no statement till you and your staff had held a private inquiry.

You were perfectly justified, but in my professional opinion Miss Kerr was not exposed to infection in this hospital and there can be no more secrecy.' Mark recalled the scratches on a child's body, and the cuts of a whip, and the strip of plaster hiding a T-shaped scar and his formality left him.

'Get on to the blower at once, Brian. Call the Home Office and the local Inspector of Health and the police.

'No, you'd better inform the police first, and after them the newspapers and the television and radio authorities. We want the maximum publicity, so tell them this.' Mark's eyes were very tired from peering at the slides and, as he looked at the dean, Plunket's features seemed to blur and shrivel and become the face of an old, old woman.

'If the man who raped Elsie Kerr is not found – and found quickly – there's every chance that one hell of an epidemic is going to break out.'

Ten

'Please take a seat, madam. Inspector Moxton won't be long.' The desk sergeant motioned Tania to a bench. As Steele had promised, a patrol car had arrived almost as soon as he rang off and rushed her to Asterford, a quiet market town with a police station that fitted the locality. The notices displayed in the reception hall were all concerned with rural pursuits: fishing rights and shotgun licences, fowl pest and Colorado beetle, strayed and stolen animals.

'They should never have let me see him, should they?' A room on her left had a badly fitting door with glass panels and Tania could see and hear a middle-aged couple being interviewed by a plainclothes man. 'I'll never get over the shock, will I? Not as long as I live.'

'I'm sure it was a most harrowing experience, madam, but if we could continue with your husband's statement.' The detective turned to the man, who had bloodshot eyes and a pronounced stubble on his receding chin. 'I understand that the pigs had not been fed for a considerable time, Mr Seaton-Osterbury.'

'Not since ten o'clock yesterday morning, officer.' The man's arms were folded and Tania suspected he had adopted the pose to hide trembling hands. 'I mean the day before yesterday, of course. I'd forgotten it was after midnight.'

'Yes, that's a very considerable period, isn't it?' The policeman looked at a sheet of typescript on his desk. 'Do you often neglect your livestock for so long, sir? Don't think I'm being impertinent, but I must know if it was common knowledge that those pigs were sometimes in a ravenous condition.'

'You don't dare answer that, dare you, Arthur?' Her husband had remained silent with his head slumped and the woman took over. 'Yes, officer, he was always forgetting to feed the animals and the whole village knows it. Why, didn't an inspector from the R.S.P.C.A. get on to him not so long ago? He's an alcoholic and an idler and he was drunk all day yesterday. That's why the beasts were kept hungry.'

'Thank you, madam.' The policeman made a marginal note. 'It was common knowledge, in fact.'

'Yes, and it'll be common knowledge what the brutes did, won't it?' The woman was bristling with fury. 'Who'll buy 'em now, do you think? Would you like a slice of corpse-fed bacon on your breakfast plate, Arthur?'

'Ah, Lady Levin.' Moxton had appeared from a corridor and held out his hand to Tania. 'I do appreciate your willingness to help us and if you would come this way—' He led her down the passage and into a room where Steele and two other men were waiting. 'May I introduce Inspector Brown of the Surrey C.I.D., and Dr Croxley, the local police surgeon. Constable Steele you know, of course.'

'How do you do, Lady Levin.' Croxley was large and elderly, with an old-fashioned black suit, and a watch-chain draped across his ample belly. 'I know your husband by reputation, naturally, and it is a great pleasure to make your acquaintance. Though I'm sorry we had to meet under such distressing circumstances.' He produced a purple silk handkerchief and blew his nose loudly. 'A horrible business and you're very public-spirited to render assistance. I must say I was astonished that a lady should be asked to make an identification.'

'Lady Levin made the offer, Doctor. We suspect that the corpse may belong to a man with few other friends and acquaintances capable of identifying him, and that is why we accepted her help.' Moxton had spoken coldly but his tone became fatherly when he turned to Tania. 'All the same we really are grateful, Lady Levin, and I do hope you won't be too distressed.'

'I'll try not to be, Inspector.' Tania recalled the conversation in the interview room. If the body was John Batterday's, as seemed likely, she had to learn all she could about his death. 'I am only too glad to help you, gentlemen, but in return would you give me the details of the case? Is it true that the man had been savaged by starving pigs?'

'Um, I'm sorry you overheard that.' Brown had moved to a cupboard and he spoke with his back towards her. 'It's true I'm afraid. The poor devil was naked apart from a blanket and he was found in a pig paddock. Naturally the animals had torn him about pretty badly.' He came towards her with a glass of brandy in his hand. 'Please drink this, Lady Levin.'

'Thank you, Inspector.' Tania disliked brandy, but she took the glass from him intending to toy with it and try to gain time and ask more questions. She felt no fears for the approaching ordeal. On the contrary she was wildly excited, because the one serious flaw in her theory about Batterday, the time factor, seemed to be solved.

John Batterday was a compulsive sadist, he might have felt guilt about his cravings, but it was not he who had destroyed the pictures. That had been done by the people who fired the shot she and Henson witnessed. Violent people – unforgiving people, who considered prison sentences inadequate punishments for rape and torture – maybe people who had criminal records and no desire to confide in the police. People who knew how locks were picked. The relatives or friends of one of Batterday's earlier victims, who had called at his house in person to make sure that their second attempt to kill him did not fail. And when they found that their quarry had flown those people would have been very angry and frustrated and Batterday's art collection had provided them with a whipping boy. 'You're very kind, Inspector.' Tania accepted a cigarette from Moxton and returned to her thoughts.

The hunters had not abandoned the chase, however. They had made inquiries, probably at hotels and travel agencies and car-hire firms, and they had tracked him down. Batterday's victims were revenged, but this was the important point. He had been found *after* the attack on Elsie Kerr.

'To be eaten alive by hungry pigs, gentlemen.' She took a sip of brandy and tried to imagine the mentality of the murderers. 'What a horrible way to die!'

'Oh, the pigs didn't kill him, my dear. Please don't think that.' Moxton hastened to reassure her. 'A reliable witness passed the paddock at four o'clock yesterday afternoon and apart from thinking the herd seemed restless, he saw nothing amiss. Dr Croxley has been quite unable to give a firm opinion on the time or cause of the man's death, but he is sure . . . fairly sure that he'd been dead long before that.'

'I resent your tone, Inspector,' Croxley broke in coldly. 'The pigs had mauled the corpse so badly that it's a wonder I could give you even a rough time estimate. I also said that a drug over-dose may have killed him. Traces of Destrophine K were present in the arteries.' He looked at Tania who had given a surprised gasp. 'Does that mean anything to you, Lady Levin?'

'Only that my husband once mentioned the preparation.' Tania replied indifferently, but the name of the drug had hardened her convictions a little more.

'What puzzles me is why there was anything left of the corpse for you to examine.' The local policeman's face showed his bewilderment. 'We know that the animals were desperately hungry, but Seaton-Osterbury claimed that when he reached the field they had stopped eating. He's not a witness I'd put much faith in, but it was the same when our chaps arrived. There wasn't a pig within yards of the corpse. The whole herd were at the other side of the field with a flock of geese screaming at 'em from beyond the railings.'

'And yet it's an efficient way to dispose of unwanted bodies: been done over here and in the States and in Europe. On each occasion the pigs hardly left a morsel of flesh or bone to identify the victim.' Moxton turned to Tania. 'Your ordeal won't be too gruesome, Lady Levin. Though the base of the skull was broken, one side of the face is not badly mutilated and that's what you'll see. Mr Brown was able to note a resemblance to Batterday's passport photograph we circularized immediately.'

'Then let's get it over with, Inspector Moxton.' Tania finished her brandy. 'I'm quite ready.'

'Excellent.' He nodded to Brown to lead the way and took Tania's elbow. The doctor and Steele followed and as they turned out of the corridor into a paved yard Tania had the ludicrous notion that she was an actress rehearsing the role of a tragedy queen. Mary Stuart or Marie Antoinette being led to the scaffold by her grieving retainers.

'Here we are, my dear.' They had reached the morgue which was a small windowless building resembling a brick-built garage and Moxton's grip tightened reassuringly while Brown unlocked the door. 'And don't worry. If the shock makes you dizzy, I'll see that you don't fall.'

'I'll be perfectly all right.' Tania walked confidently into the room. Her sole anxiety was that a mistake had been made and a stranger's body would be shown to her, but she felt sure the worry was needless. It was John Batterday who had been placed in the pig field and Mark would be in the clear as soon as she told her companions the whole story.

The dead man lay sideways on a trestle table and a plastic sheet stretched from his feet to his chin. A naked light bulb gave the face a harsh, shiny pallor which was far more pronounced than that of any corpse Tania had seen, and it appeared tiny; a wax image waiting for the painter's brush to provide colour and the semblance of life. Part of the lower lip was missing, but as Moxton had promised, the features – at least the side of the features which was turned towards her – were not badly damaged. They looked like Batterday's, they looked like Mark's, but they appeared so shrunken, so completely dead, that she just couldn't picture them ever belonging to a living human being.

The features were Batterday's, though. She recognized the curve of the nose now, the sweep of the hairline, the lobe of an ear. It was just the glaring light that made the face appear so small and inhuman and there was a simple way to make a firm identification.

'I'm almost sure it's John Batterday, Inspector. But to be certain I need to see the rest of the body.'

'Thank you.' Tania was perfectly calm as Brown pulled down the sheet and the hideous wounds produced by teeth and jaws and a scalpel were revealed. But then quite suddenly . . . without the least warning, the light bulb flickered, the floor swung sideways, and if Moxton had not held her she would have toppled forward on to the poor mangled body.

'You're sure you're feeling better, my dear? Quite yourself again?' Inspector Moxton repeated the questions for the fifth time since they had started the journey back to London. Though a scourge to criminals, he was a kindly, paternal man and had three daughters of about Tania's age.

'I'm fine thanks to you, Inspector. Just ashamed that I behaved so hysterically.' Now that her sudden fear had been proved groundless Tania was in complete control of herself, though the shock of seeing those hands would haunt her for a long time. Unscarred hands which could not have belonged to Batterday, but might be Mark's.

But everything was all right. As soon as she'd come out of the brief coma and explained its cause the inspector had proved a real friend. He had immediately telephoned St Bede's and threatened the receptionist with dire penalties if he was not connected with somebody in authority. In a minute or two he was speaking to Brian Plunket and after a brief silence he handed Tania the phone and she heard Mark's voice.

'Darling, what on earth's going on? They tell me you're somewhere in Surrey.' He had seemed preoccupied and cut her short when she started to explain in detail. 'Look, Tania, I can only stay a moment because we're up to our eyes here, so ask the police to drive you home and then try to get some sleep.' He had broken off and she had heard the dean urging him to be brief. 'I really must go, but I'll be home just as soon as I possibly can.'

'Oh, that business.' She had asked him about the rape accusations and he had sounded almost surprised, as if it had completely slipped his mind. 'Don't give that a thought, Tania. There's nothing to worry about on that score and I'll explain when I see you. Goodbye, my darling.' He had blown a kiss down the line and hung up.

'I'm just sorry I couldn't help you, Inspector.' Tania stared out of the car window. The storm had completely passed and the early-morning sky seemed to promise a fine day. 'I felt practically certain the man was Batterday till I saw his hands.'

'You've helped us a good deal.' Steele was driving and Moxton sat beside her in the back. 'I might have wasted a lot of time on account of a superficial facial resemblance if you hadn't reminded me that Batterday always wore gloves to conceal disfiguring scars and pointed out that there was no old scar tissue on the hands of the corpse.

'Apart from a skin complaint or disfigurement there's only one reason why a man should habitually wear gloves: to screen his fingers because he had a record and was wanted by the police.' Moxton pulled out his cigarettes and lit one for himself when Tania refused. 'Well, the corpse's fingerprints are not on file and, as you know, we didn't find a single print in Batterday's house. That seems to prove that his story about the scars was true and we'll have to look for the joker elsewhere.' He grinned at Steele through the driving mirror. 'Which is a pity, eh, Alf?'

'You can say that again, sir.' The constable replied with feeling. 'Being on the team of a spectacular murder investigation is one of the best ladders to promotion, Lady Levin.'

'Not to worry, son.' Moxton grunted cheerfully. 'There's still the matter of the pictures to be sorted out, so let's just hope that the boffins are right.'

'That murder was certainly spectacular.' The word made Tania think of what she had seen in the morgue and she hardly heard Moxton's last sentence. 'What sort of mind could have thought of such a way to dispose of a body?'

'That'll be for the Surrey Police or Scotland Yard to discover, because we're off the case, I'm sorry to say. But whoever that corpse belonged to, he'd made some pretty unpleasant enemies. Cunning ones too, though I can think of better ways to get rid of him.' The car had stopped at a traffic signal and Moxton nodded towards a motorway running across the road. 'There's a villain buried inside one of those arches, as a matter of fact. Jimmy

Balchin, who organized the Newcastle bank raid three years ago. His grateful pals slung him into a concrete mixer while the road was being built. We know Jimmy's there, we know who put him there, but we can hardly tear down the whole damn flyover to fish out the little that's left of him.'

'The pigs weren't a bad idea, though, sir.' The lights had changed and Steele let in the clutch. 'If the thunder hadn't frightened them off there'd have been precious little left of the body you saw, Lady Levin.'

'I just can't understand that, gentlemen. Would a storm, or anything else for that matter, keep animals away from food if they were really hungry? I'd have thought one would have to beat them off the body.'

'Yes, that's what Inspector Brown thought, and it does seem strange, though I'm no countryman and animals are a closed book to me. The local police have a pretty shrewd idea why the pigs were unfed, though.' Moxton pulled thoughtfully at his cigarette.

'The farmer, Seaton . . . Seaton . . . I can't remember the rest of his damn name, was a drunk who'd often neglected his livestock in the past. But some while back an R.S.P.C.A. inspector gave him merry hell. Scared the daylights out of him and as far as the animals were concerned he'd been a fairly reformed character till yesterday. So why did he go and blot his copybook on the very day that someone had an unwanted stiff to dispose of?' He paused and frowned at Tania. 'Officially I suppose I shouldn't be telling you this, my dear, so don't let it go any further.

'Apparently, Seaton had a hangover most mornings and it was his habit to call at the pub at opening time, have one drink – a strong light ale – to steady his nerves, and then go back to work. But before he'd finished his drink a man and a woman got into conversation with him and bought him another. They were strangers to the village, just passing through by car, but the barmaid said they treated Seaton as though he was a long-lost brother. The woman, a flashy, ginger-haired type, buttered him up no end, and the man kept standing him refills and insisting he laced the beer with Scotch.'

'They got him drunk to see that he'd forget to feed the pigs

... to ensure that the animals would be ravenous. Yes, that is cunning. Inspector, devilishly cunning.' They were crossing a bridge, below them a tugboat whistled shrilly as it approached the arch, and Tania thought of a girl's screams. 'Daddy . . . Daddy . . . Devil Daddy.' Elsie Kerr loved reading, and *Wuthering Heights* was one of her favourite books. Most probably the quotation had slipped out automatically, but if that was not so . . . if Elsie had used the term because it was appropriate, the suggestion was that her rape had been motivated by something more sinister than physical lust.

She was theorizing again. She had too much imagination, as Mark often told her, and she was letting it run riot. Tania set the notion aside and listened to what the policemen were saying.

'But the jokers weren't so cunning leaving that blanket behind sir, and it might nail them in the end. They couldn't drive a car to the paddock, the body had to be covered by something, but why not use canvas or sacking. A gaudy, hand-woven thing like that cries out for its makers to be traced, and I bet they will be.'

'Agreed, Alf.' The inspector nodded. 'Though I don't think *blanket*'s the proper description; more like a bedspread or a light quilt. And all those colours and embroidered symbols. Native work, would you say?'

'Hardly that, sir.' Steele swung the car on to the Richmond Road. 'The symbols, if that's what they are, looked European to me. Remember those things like the letter "T" forming the margin and the numerals in the centre. A cluster of half a dozen number sixes set in a sort of curlicue.'

'That's true, Alf. But what's the matter, my dear?' Tania had gasped and Moxton looked concerned. 'Not feeling faint again, are you?'

'No, I'm all right, Inspector.' The letter T, Tania thought. A cross without a head-piece. A mark like that had been branded on the girl's forehead. 'But don't you understand what the symbols could mean, gentlemen? Thirty-six – Six sixes is the Number of the Beast.'

'Sorry, I'm not with you.' The inspector wound down a window to give her air. 'What animal would that be?'

'The creature from the pit; the Beast of the Apocalypse, of

course. Saint John describes it in his *Revelation* and its separate identities were depicted in that big canvas of Batterday's. The one showing six creatures in a cave. The Dragon, the Whore, the . . .'

'Ah yes, the picture that had been stubbed with cigarette ends.' The inspector pulled out his memo book. ' "After the school of Hieronymus Bosch, the fifteenth-century Dutch painter, by a contemporary copyist; possibly a student of the master." ' He read his notes aloud. 'When you suggested that Batterday might deal in faked pictures I got two of our art experts to have a look at the remains of the collection and they became rather excited.'

'I suppose they found the pictures were modern fakes?'

'On the contrary, they suspect that the whole collection is stolen property. Anger at the destruction that had been done was their first reaction, wasn't it, Alf?'

'You can say that again, sir.' Steele grinned. 'I'd never seen a man actually tear his hair before, but that's what Inspector Jacobson did.'

'Yes, he was very upset indeed and he may have had reason to be.' Though the dawn was breaking it was still too dark to read with comfort and Moxton switched on an interior light. 'Exhaustive tests will have to be made, of course, but according to Jacobson and his colleague, those pictures would have been worth . . .' He turned a page of the notebook. 'Something in the region of half a million pounds.'

Eleven

'Sorry about that interruption.' Mark had returned to the conference room after speaking to Tania on the telephone and he faced his audience once more. The dean had not taken his advice to publicize the situation immediately, but officialdom had been summoned from its bed, arriving at the hospital in several frames of mind, all of them hostile.

Surgeon-General Cranleigh of the army research station at Dorking was openly furious at the early-morning call. Commander Trant of Scotland Yard had stated that the Kerr investigation was in the capable hands of a colleague and no affair of his. Miss Glendower, the Home Office representative, and Mr Howard, the press liaison officer, were almost half asleep, while Lord Aikenhead from the Ministry of Health appeared to be slightly intoxicated.

But nobody was angry or asleep or fuddled now, and while Mark was out of the room they had welcomed the opportunity to look at the photographs again and gather their thoughts. Just two photographs had sufficed to change their moods. One of a pretty blonde girl in a bathing costume. One of an old woman's body. That had been enough to leave Mark's audience shaken and silent and cold sober and on his return he could see anxiety on every face.

'You know what the disease did to one individual human being, ladies and gentlemen, and I presume you can appreciate what might happen if it became epidemic.' He waited for a murmur of agreement to die down and nodded to Paul Johnston, stationed by a slide projector.

'We shall now give you an idea how the illness progressed.' The lights dimmed and an image glowed on a screen. 'That shows a sample of arterial blood photographed through a microscope shortly before Miss Kerr's death.' Mark raised a ruler to the screen. 'As you can see, there is no indication that the corpuscles were attacked by any micro-organism. They are not diseased;

merely senile, as was to be expected. When the picture was taken Miss Kerr had all the physical characteristics of a woman aged between eighty-five and ninety-five years.

'So, take a look at the beast responsible.' The blood specimen had been viewed in silence, but the next slide brought a stronger reaction. General Cranleigh snorted, Miss Glendower's chair creaked as she leaned forward, Lord Aikenhead gave an astonished gasp.

'This is a section of pituitary tissue removed immediately after death and it gives you a glimpse of the creature that in less than thirty hours turned a young girl into a crone.' The ruler tapped a cluster of star-shaped objects on the screen. They were very blurred and indistinct, and when he had first spotted them under the microscope Mark had thought of a shadowy universe; stars and planets and moons viewed through frosted glass.

'Sorry about the poor quality of the picture, but that's the only group we were able to isolate effectively. The rest of the invaders were obliterated by the antibiotic; after the damage was done and the child doomed.' Mark traced the fissures and hillocks he had once compared to the rubbish dumps of an encamped army. 'However, there's no doubt how the gland itself was affected by the parasite's presence. The metabolism has altered, the cellular structure is out of balance, the whole unit is . . . is deformed. Please excuse such vague and unscientific terms, ladies and gentlemen, but I can't think of any better descriptions.' Mark rubbed his free hand across his chin. He was unshaven, his eyes were red and aching, and he felt mentally exhausted.

'And life was terminated in a matter of hours.' Lord Aikenhead had sobered up and the slight slur in his voice was not due to alcohol, but worry. 'What is the organism, Levin? A virus or bacillus?'

'We can rule out both those species. The next exhibit proves that.' Mark nodded to Paul Johnston again and a line of needle-like objects was displayed. 'These were located in one of the sweat glands and they appear to be the enemy's weapons. Spears and arrows to penetrate the body of a host. Cupid's arrows, one might say. Darts containing the protoplasm by which the creature reproduces itself.'

'You mean spores?' General Cranleigh had been less shaken than the others and he stood up to take a closer look at the screen. 'That suggests the agent is fungoid, but surely the second slide ruled that out, Levin?'

'Quite correct, General. The creature acts in a similar manner and has the characteristics of certain fungi. At first I thought it was something related to *acinomycosis* or *Streptothra madura*, but that was before I saw the enlargement of the pituitary specimen.' He motioned Johnston to turn on the lights. 'The thing is not a true fungus, it's not like any germ or micro-organism that's been classified and we're still working in the dark. If only the Genomycin had left a few survivors, so that we could grow cultures and study the creatures under proper laboratory conditions . . .' He shrugged and returned to his seat at a table beside Plunket. 'I just don't know what we're up against and that's why I asked you to be present, Cranleigh. The establishment under your command is engaged in germ warfare research.'

'It is indeed, and very effectively too.' The general nodded self-importantly. 'So, you suspect that the agent might be an artificially-produced mutation.' He peered at the picture still glowing on the screen.

'Possible – yes. Probable – no. I can't tell you what line of research our Soviet competitors are following at the moment, but to produce a biological weapon one uses well-classified micro-organisms with stable life-cycles. We have to know how the little brutes will react when we mess them about.' He paused, considering how much information it was proper to divulge.

'One method is to breed selectively from an age-old enemy, such as the bubonic plague bacillus, till the new strains become virtually unstoppable; resistant to human antibodies and chemical drugs.

'You can also alter the habits of a species that only preys on plants or animals. Parrot disease, for example, is a most adaptable chap, who can easily be persuaded to change his choice of victim, and the human system has no defence against him.' Cranleigh sat down and shook his head emphatically. 'No, Levin, I'm pretty sure we haven't got a man-made mutant to worry about.'

'Then it's a natural form of life.' Megan Glendower, the Home

Office representative, spoke hesitantly. 'Sir Marcus, could the organism belong to a genus that was formerly a scourge, and then degenerated? Lain dormant for centuries, long before the invention of the microscope, and now started to regain its powers and come into the open once more? I've heard that influenza strains have behaved like that.'

'Possibly, Miss Glendower.' Brian Plunket answered to give Mark a break. 'Certain spore-producing bacteria can remain dormant but alive almost indefinitely and then germinate and reproduce themselves when climatic conditions are favourable. But though your suggestion is feasible we can say no more than that.' He leaned forward across the table. 'The important thing – the really vital thing, madam – is to find the original source of the infection, and waste no time in doing so.'

'You . . . you mean the man who . . .' She had not realized the implications till now and her head jerked back as though he had struck her. '. . . who attacked Elsie Kerr.'

'Exactly, and that is why you were all sent for so hurriedly. The spores which transmit the illness are contained in the sweat glands, but Sir Marcus considers it unlikely that they can penetrate the human skin. Direct entry into the bloodstream would be needed.'

'And that's why he called them "Cupid's arrows". The girl was infected while the rape occurred – when he clawed at her, or when he broke the hymen.' Miss Glendower's voice was shrill and hysterical.

'So what we've got is an immune carrier on the rampage. A man with a complaint that does not trouble him because his own antibodies hold it in check. But he can pass on the parasite to others who have no resistance and . . . and . . .' She glanced wildly around the room as if imagining Elsie Kerr's attacker might be present, though neither she nor anyone else could possibly suspect Mark now. It was a Mr Unknown who filled their thoughts. A vague, shadowy figure as mysterious as the poison he carried in his body.

'And that man is a maniac . . . a crazed animal who attacks children, and at this very moment . . . while we're sitting here . . . another girl may be struggling against his tainted body . . . growing old and ill in his arms.'

'Take it easy, Miss Glendower.' The Scotland Yard Commander, who was sitting next to her, laid a reassuring hand on her wrist. 'We'll find the joker all right, but it may take time, unless we get the fullest cooperation from the public.' He rounded on Lord Aikenhead, and Howard, the press officer.

'Gentlemen, there's no time to spare, is there, and it's up to you to see that we get that cooperation. I don't have to tell you that sexual offenders often go free because friends and relatives screen them.' Trant mimicked a woman's cockney accent. '"Pore dear 'Arry never meant no 'arm – the little bitch led the boy on. 'Arry couldn't 'elp 'imself, so let's keep quiet about the blood on 'is jacket."'

'That's the kind of attitude which holds us back in rape cases from time to time, but nobody's going to screen this bastard, if you lay on the publicity good and thick. I want the Ministry of Health to issue a statement on the radio and television emphasizing the gravity of the situation, Lord Aikenhead. I want you, Mr Howard, to make sure that the full story, and the photographs we have seen, appear in every newspaper – national and provincial.'

'One moment please.' Howard had nodded eagerly, but Aikenhead frowned. 'While agreeing that the matter is urgent, such publicity would almost certainly cause public unrest, if not panic, and I have a question to ask.' He looked at Mark and Plunket. 'You consider that the man we want has developed immunity to a horrible disease and can pass it on to others. But to be guilty of rape he must be an adult, or at least a teenage youth, so why have no other cases of the illness been reported in the past?'

'A good point, sir.' The dean inclined his head. 'Even if this was the fellow's first sexual assault, he is bound to have made scores of other physical contacts capable of spreading the complaint. He must have touched people with cuts and sores and chapped hands and so forth. Why weren't they infected?'

'Exactly, Doctor, and that suggests that the man himself only contracted the disease recently. If so, he would have suffered some alarming symptoms before developing immunity. That is always the case with diphtheria and typhus carriers, and he may have sought medical advice.' Aikenhead gave Commander

Trant a hard stare. 'Before any alarmist statements are issued I intend to have details of the illness circulated to every hospital, nursing home and general practitioner in the country, and find out whether any man suffering from an unusual glandular disturbance has been treated by them during the last two months.'

'Are you out of your mind, sir?' . . . 'It would take days before the answers came in.' . . . 'Don't you realize the urgency, man?' Trant and Howard and the general were beside themselves with anger, but Mark remained silent and his eyes were fixed on the screen. Aikenhead's point was valid, as Plunket had said, and it was exceedingly strange that Elsie Kerr had been the first victim reported. But somehow he just did not believe that her attacker had been recently infected. He was also quite certain that no doctor had examined him, though he had no concrete reasons for his belief.

'I demand that the statement is issued . . .' 'I do not accept demands unless they come from my minister, Commander.' Aikenhead and Trant were shouting at each other, but Mark was hardly conscious of their voices and he raised his own to attract Johnston's attention. 'Put the second slide on again, Paul, and turn off the lights.'

Just what was the creature? His heartbeats quickened as the star-shaped objects reappeared. Not a virus . . . not a bacillus . . . not a fungus. And if Cranleigh was right, not a mutation. So what on earth could it be?

The sudden darkness had silenced Trant and Aikenhead, everyone was waiting for an explanation, but Mark remained silent and all at once he remembered his words when he and William Travers had decided to abandon the rejection control experiments. 'We've had it, Will. The antibodies contained in the foreign tissue thrive too successfully and all we're achieving is the destruction of large numbers of inoffensive animals.'

Could that sentence contain the secret? Were the things he was staring at not parasites – not germs at all? Not even enemies, but friendly allies? The guardians of health which only turned rogue when passed into a strange environment. Possibly, but they bore small resemblance to any human antibodies he had seen and he dreaded voicing his suspicions in public. All the same he had to voice them because, if they were correct, merry hell was about to break out.

'Lights please, Paul.' He faced his audience with a deep sense of embarrassment. 'Ladies and gentlemen, I have just been considering a possibility and you may think it a damn silly one. If you do, I won't blame you in the slightest.' Mark Levin prided himself on his assurance and self-confidence, but at that moment he felt like a nervous student before an examining board . . . an applicant pleading for a badly needed job.

'A parasite that can only be located in one part of the body, in this case the glandular system, is a scientific freak. The illness responsible for Elsie Kerr's senility progressed far more rapidly and acted quite differently from any natural disease cycle that has been isolated and described, but General Cranleigh is confident that the organism was not produced artificially and we must accept his judgment.'

'Damnation!' Mark was longing for more time to gather his thoughts and he got it from Plunket. An intercom whirred hoarsely and the dean reached for the switch. 'Excuse me a second.'

'Miss Percy, how many times must I repeat that we are accepting no more calls? Oh, so Professor Henson is with you and he wants to know why I have placed the hospital in a state of security. He insists on knowing, does he?' Plunket clearly shared Mark's feelings towards Henson. 'Well, give the Professor my compliments and tell him to go and boil his head.' He switched off the set and nodded to Mark. 'Please continue.'

'Miss Glendower . . . gentlemen.' During the brief interval Mark's suspicions had grown a little stronger, but he still felt ill at ease and far from confident. 'I am merely groping in the dark, but is it possible that Elsie Kerr was not infected by a germ or a parasite, but by a defence unit? An antibody passed into her system by a man who was not a carrier of disease, but a perfectly healthy individual?

'If that is correct, there is a simple, though rather flamboyant answer to your query, Lord Aikenhead. No other cases of the illness have been reported because Elsie's attacker only came to this country a few days ago.

'No, not a foreigner in the general sense of the term, and I was wrong to call him a man.' Almost everybody in the room had burst out with the same question, but it was General Cranleigh's opinion Mark wanted and he looked him hard in the eyes. 'I wonder if the child was attacked by someone ... something who has recently arrived from outer space and whose alien genes killed her.'

'When ... just when will the revelation begin ... how long before we start to feel his power?' The old woman in the wheelchair was very frail; she looked almost as old as Elsie Kerr had done shortly before her death and she suffered badly from bronchitis. The words left her lips in agonized gasps. 'When will I be able to leave this chair and walk ... to breathe the air freely again?'

'Have no fear, dear lady.' The group were assembled in the big brown room and Canon Hamilton smiled from one face to another. To the millionaire industrialist and the photographer, to a postman and a dentist, to the housewife and the mechanic and a schoolteacher. Some of his listeners were elderly, some young, but the majority were middle-aged and they were drawn from all strata of society. The Canon himself was a man of comfortable means now, but he had gone through some hard times in the past, and had been working as a barman when the millionaire recognized his value and provided him with a stipend. 'None of us need have any fear because the one who leads us did not lie. The man was what we believed him to be; the Keeper of the door – the Wanderer – the Hunter, and his powers will soon be passed over to us.' The canon had substituted his elaborate robes for a plain black cassock, but he looked just as impressive as when he had conducted the service.

'The promise will be kept, the revelation will take place, because we have done all things which were ordained. The obscene depictions he hoarded were mocked and disfigured ... the ceremonies were performed in exact ritual ... the vessel of grace was filled ... the flesh and the blood have been consumed. Before long we will feel the touch of our master's hand and be rewarded.' He genuflected towards a large oil painting that dominated the room. In style it was rather similar to Dali's *Crucifixion* and showed a young man plunging head-first through an evening sky. 'It was he who prompted the Wanderer to commit the greatest act of his life. It was he who ordered us to release him.'

'You are right of course, Father.' The bank manager spoke from the window. Behind his back a pale moon was still visible, though the sun was climbing over London. 'But why is there no news of the chalice; the holy vessel that had to be filled and desecrated, but not mortally harmed?'

'Yes, that is peculiar – worrying too, and I'm not a man given to needless worries. Still, our host should have news for us by now.' The millionaire consulted his watch and turned to the housewife, who was manicuring her nails. 'You and Marsden carried out your part of the operation to the letter, Mrs Danvers?'

'We did exactly what we were told to do.' She looked at the mechanic for confirmation. 'Isn't that true, George?'

'Course it's true. We didn't put a foot wrong, Sir Roland, you can count on that. And for the life of me, I can't see what anybody's got to worry about. Canon Hamilton said it would take time for the effects to be felt, so let's all relax.' There was a sound of tyres on gravel and he grinned cheerfully. 'That'll be the news we're waiting for, and you mark my words, nowt's gone wrong and there's nowt to worry about.' He strode across to the bank manager and they pulled open the windows as the car stopped and the driver got out.

'Well?' said the dentist, as their host stepped into the room . . . 'What's the news?' shrilled the housewife . . . 'Out with it, man,' demanded the industrialist . . . 'Is anything wrong?' wheezed the old woman, propelling her chair across the carpet. They all jostled eagerly around him, but once they realized what the man's expression might mean they drew back as though he were a leper.

'There's no news at all,' he answered after a long silence. 'But I think we may be in trouble – dead trouble.'

Twelve

'I was such a fool, darling. The room seemed to go dark, my legs gave way and I fainted.' Tania poured out more coffee. 'Everything suggested that the man was John Batterday; the drug he'd taken, the destruction of the pictures, the way his murderers had tried to get rid of the body. I was sure he'd been killed in revenge for raping some other girl or woman. Then, when I realized it couldn't possibly be John, I thought I was looking at you, Mark.'

'You might have passed out if you'd known the man was a complete stranger from the start.' They were sitting on a sofa in Mark's library and he put an arm around her shoulder. 'A badly mutilated corpse could make anyone feel faint and the police had no right to ask you to look at it.

'But do try to forget what you saw and in return I'll promise to let no pig so much as nibble me.' Mark tried to speak lightly, but he felt incapable of humour and knew that the joke was a poor one. Though he had had a bath and a couple of hours sleep since getting home he was still mentally drained and frustration racked him like an ulcer. For the time being he was completely useless. Till Elsie Kerr's attacker was arrested or another of his victims provided him with more data to examine there was nothing to do but wait and fret and worry. Lord Aikenhead had still not issued his statement to the public and very shortly a great many people might be consumed by tiny animals which were far more voracious than pigs.

'And the police are now certain John Batterday was an art thief, or at least a receiver?' Mark had reassured Tania that he was no longer under any suspicion of rape, but only given her a rough account of the medical threat looming over everyone. He wanted to forget it himself till a summons from Trant or some other official gave him the signal to resume work. But however much he tried to concentrate on Tania's story he missed a great deal of what she said because Elsie Kerr and the things that had withered her kept nagging at his brain.

If Elsie had not caught the infection during a brutal attack, but through some innocent encounter, she would have felt quite well for several hours and been as lethal as a time bomb. Mark imagined the girl preparing a meal for her family – sweat might pass on the illness. He saw her kissing a boy-friend – it was unlikely that the actual breath could transmit the spores, but the salivary glands housed them and direct oral contact would probably do so. He saw her shaking hands with somebody who had an open cut or a graze. He pictured her in half a dozen situations, all of them deadly.

The opportunities for those tiny spores to spread were legion, and before the first symptoms of the malaise appeared Elsie could have claimed several victims. They in their turn would infect just as many more and the disease accelerate unchecked, because mankind had no inborn resistance against the unfamiliar enemy. The human defences were programmed to destroy parasites they had met before; germs responsible for cholera, plague, the common cold and all other earthly illnesses. They had no weapons, and possibly no inclination, to fight the alien invaders because they were fellow antibodies and kindred spirits. The guardians of a hostile camp who had gone over to the offensive.

And unless that camp ... unless the carrier who had caused Elsie's illness was located quickly ... unless massive supplies of antibiotics were built up and distributed before he struck again and the attack gathered momentum, Mark had no doubts about the future. The world would be in for a pandemic as disastrous as the Black Death.

'A little green man with bug eyes and antenna-like ears, Sir Marcus.' Tania was telling him about the cloth found beside the body, but Lord Aikenhead's sneers were fresh in his memory. 'Come – come, ladies and gentlemen. I can credit the possibility that life on other planets may be more advanced than we are. But I cannot believe in a space visitor with sexual leanings towards our own fair sex. Pirates and other terrestrial voyagers have frequently ravished native women, but Martians ... I ask you.'

The galling thing was that the jibes were probably justified. As soon as he had voiced them openly Mark had begun to lose faith in his theories and he knew that they had entered his mind because he was so completely out of his depth. All he did know was that the organism in question resembled nothing recorded by medical history and it had to be studied and rendered harmless.

But though Aikenhead had sneered and repeated his anxieties about public unrest and panic, he and Cranleigh and Trant had forced him to compromise. There was no time to question private doctors and nursing homes, but at the moment the Ministry of Health's telephone exchange was busily contacting every major hospital in the country. If no case of an unknown glandular condition had been reported to them during the last week, the facts would be made public.

'A pattern of entwined sixes and a border formed by a line of "T" shapes. That's what made you consider the cloth might be some sort of ceremonial shroud, Tania?' Mark withdrew his arm from her shoulder and reached for a cigarette. 'Look, my sweet, being a Yid, I'm not a great reader of the New Testament, but I do know that six sixes symbolize the Beast of the Apocalypse. Also, you told me that Henson considered the "Tau" cross – a headless cross like the letter "T" – was once an anti-Christian symbol denoting a god who has lost his powers and no longer controls the universe. But I do wish you wouldn't brood on the Satanic coven possibilities. It's so nonsensical – unhealthy too.' Mark lit the cigarette and forced his own preoccupations aside. He was worried about Tania, who had had a horrible experience and was a very imaginative woman. The police should never have accepted her offer to view the body, and they appeared to be not only inconsiderate but inefficient as well. None of Batterday's pictures was listed in any reference book or catalogue, but two so-called art experts considered that the collection contained original works by Bosch, Dürer and Goya and was worth half a million pounds. A ludicrous suggestion, because how could Batterday have got hold of such things? From where had they been stolen and why had the thefts not been publicized? Also who in his senses would keep priceless masterpieces in a suburban bungalow, even if it had anti-burglar locks? Mark himself had suspected that one of the Dürer reproductions might be genuine when he first saw it, but only for a fleeting instant. The police experts must have imaginations even more vivid than Tania's.

'But one thing puzzles me, darling. The doctor considered that the man whose body you saw could have died from a drug overdose. Why did that make you connect him with John Batterday? John certainly isn't a drug addict.'

'I never thought he was, Mark. What I did wonder was if he might use drugs at rare intervals. You see, Dr Croxley found Destrophine K in the bloodstream and you once described the symptoms to me.'

'Which are hallucinations – religious mania – delusions of power. Destrophine's a real killer and it was very properly taken off the market last year.' Mark was interested at last. 'Yes, I see your line of reasoning. A morally sound man troubled by perverted sexual desires might repress them with . . . how can I put it? Surroundings – mechanical devices? Pictures reminding him of hellfire, a bedroom like a hermit's cell, even a hair shirt and a penile ring. He could deliberately rack himself with guilts, but at times his cravings become so strong that they have to be satisfied. But, before that happens, he must discard his guilts and moralities for a period, and half a grain of Destrophine K would soon send them packing. For several hours he'd be a megalomaniac, completely convinced that all laws, divine or man-made, did not apply to himself.' The radio was switched on in readiness for Lord Aikenhead's announcement, and though the volume was turned low a wail of violin strings stirred Mark's memory and brought a cry of human anguish to his mind.

'I once examined a theological student who took a shot of Destrophine, Tania. Under its influence he'd become convinced that he was Jesus Christ and announced the fact in a public lavatory. When one of his hearers pointed out that he was uncircumcized, and consequently a liar, the boy remedied the failing then and there with a rusty penknife.' Mark lifted his cup and took a sip of coffee. 'Blood poisoning set in and complete castration was needed to save his life.

'Oh, darling, if only your hunch had been right. If that man in Surrey had been John Batterday, we'd be half-way out of the wood and I wouldn't be sitting here waiting for that fool Aikenhead. Paul Johnston and I could be at work finding out what the bug is – where it comes from – how he picked it up.' Mark raised the cup again but held it suspended before his lips as a thought struck him. 'Tania, I wasn't concentrating on what you were saying at first, but I don't think you told me why you and the police were so convinced that the body could not be Batterday's.'

'Because Batterday's hands were scarred; that's why he always wore gloves, and the hands of the corpse had no old scar tissue at all.

'But what is it, Mark? Are you ill, darling?' He had sprung up from the sofa, the cup had fallen from his hand and his eyes were bright with excitement. 'You look as if you've seen a ghost.'

'What I've seen is the truth, darling.' He pulled her up into his arms and kissed her hard on the mouth. 'Thanks to you, we're out of the dark, or soon should be. But what a fool – what a blind, stupid fool I've been.

'Now let's start the wheels turning.' He reached out for the telephone extension and dialled a number. 'Scotland Yard? My name is Sir Marcus Levin and it is imperative that I speak to Commander Trant immediately.' He was asked to hold the line and while he waited he heard the radio music fade and an announcer's voice introduce Lord Aikenhead. This was the moment Mark had been waiting for, but the statement no longer seemed important because Tania had told him all that he and the public needed to know.

The corpse was John Batterday's . . . John Batterday had raped and beaten Elsie under the influence of Destrophine . . . John Batterday might or might not have come from outer space; he might have come from anywhere, but one thing was clear . . . Batterday had had very human and very humanitarian reasons for wearing gloves.

'Will you help Redfern to do the honours, Mrs Danvers?' The owner of the house nodded towards a sideboard. 'I don't feel capable of pouring out a drink, though I can certainly use one.'

'So can we all, but there is no need to behave like a pack of neurotic schoolchildren.' The millionaire watched the housewife unstopper a bottle. 'The lack of news is disturbing, but probably means nothing.'

'Of course it don't!' As usual the mechanic sounded cheerful but he spoke to reassure himself as much as his companions. 'All the same, make mine a large scotch, Mrs D. . . . a really large one.'

'You are towers of strength, gentlemen.' The old woman in the wheelchair took a glass of sherry from the manservant's tray. 'Thank you, Redfern. All the same, I would have thought that by now at least one or two of us would be experiencing some change and the secrecy is worrying. Nothing can have gone wrong I suppose, dear Canon Hamilton?'

'I can only repeat that we followed His orders, madam. The instructions I heard in my vision were carried out in exact detail.' The canon was facing the painting of the fallen man. 'The being we freed was once His disciple who made a brave and noble gesture. But over the years he became degenerate, and it was our mission to restore him to our master's favour. We have done that . . . we have released his tired spirit and filled the chalice. His powers will soon be ours, so what is there to fear?'

'That the chalice may have been broken.' The housewife poured herself a glass of brandy. 'What if that had happened, Canon?'

'Disaster possibly, but how could it have happened? The vessel was scourged and marked with His symbol, but left in no danger.' Hamilton turned to their host. 'You confirmed that, I remember.'

'Quite true, Canon, but I can't help worrying.' The newcomer's hand trembled as he lifted a glass. 'Why are they holding back information? It was rumoured that the child was ill, but why does everybody refuse to give details? Why the secrecy?'

'It could mean that the police suspect the truth.' The housewife sipped at the brandy balloon, her lipstick leaving a thick smear on the glass. 'Suspect us?'

'Most unlikely in my opinion, and I agree with Sir Roland that we must keep calm.' The bank manager bowed deferentially to the millionaire and then looked at his watch. 'But it's time for the news, so switch on the radio, Redfern. There might be a reference to the matter.'

'Do you understand the situation, ladies and gentlemen? Have

I made myself clear?' The bank manager's watch was slow and Lord Aikenhead was half-way through his announcement. 'The police are not looking for an ordinary criminal. The person who attacked Elsie Kerr is not merely a sexual maniac, but a danger to public health.' Aikenhead paused to clear his throat.

'I have described how the child died, and those of you with television sets have seen photographs of her taken before and after her admission to St Bede's hospital. The second was not a very pleasant picture was it, so if any of you . . .' The next pause was to heighten the effect of his appeal. '. . . a parent or a child – a wife or a lover – a relative or a friend, are shielding this man I beg . . . I demand that you come forward.

'And not only in the interests of justice . . . not only to protect his future victims, but for your own safety and the safety of countless other human beings.' At the third pause there was a sharp crack as the brandy balloon shattered in the housewife's grasp.

'The person we have to find is a germ carrier . . . the spreader of a terrible illness, and Sir Marcus Levin, one of the world's most eminent bacteriologists, believes this illness could become epidemic. To make sure you appreciate how grave the position is I shall show you those photographs again and describe Miss Kerr's symptoms.'

'Lies – lies – lies.' The voices drowned the loudspeaker. 'They suspect us – they hope to panic us – they're trying to trick us – to drive us into the open.'

'But if they're not lies – if you're the liar and he's speaking the truth.' The housewife had a deep cut in her palm and blood dribbled on to the carpet as she moved from the sideboard. 'You bastard – you stupid, reckless, irresponsible bastard.' Her hand swung out like a flail and the broken glass smashed across Canon Hamilton's eyes.

Thirteen

The forged passport proved that John Batterday had been a wanderer who rarely remained long in one place. During his travels he had contracted this rare disease, but in a mild form, and his system had grown immune to its effects, though he remained a danger to others. That was why he tried to practise chastity, why he wore gloves and kept his house so spotlessly antiseptic.

Tania was in the library browsing aimlessly around the shelves while she considered Mark's suppositions. The Asterford corpse had been rushed to Central Laboratories and Mark and Paul Johnston were at work again. They were lucky. They had factual evidence to examine and, if all went well, they would arrive at a definite conclusion. All she could do was to theorize.

Most probably Mark was right in principle, she thought. When John Batterday's health recovered he had picked up a partner for the night. She might have been young or mature, dark or fair, a prostitute or an amateur, but her identity was unimportant. Only her end had significance.

They had slept together in both senses of the word, and when morning came Batterday found that his lady of the night had left the bed and an old dying woman lay gasping beside him. He would have made himself scarce and corpses are not always reported to the authorities if they die in cities like Calcutta or Cairo or Hong Kong; nor in the East End of London, if it came to that. The body must have been cold and the organisms which killed it dead and harmless before it was found. Nobody would have been very interested . . . nobody except John Batterday. He had a wide knowledge of medicine and he must have realized that his touch was responsible.

So far, so good, Tania considered, but two problems remained. Mark believed that Batterday's sadism had been caused by repression. He craved women, but shunned them for their own safety. Such a constant and unsatisfied craving might have made him resent the objects of desire and after a syringe had forced the drug

into his vein . . . after all moral considerations faded, hatred and
lust were joined together and Batterday became a monster.

A far-fetched notion; more worthy of Henson than Mark, in
Tania's opinion, and Lord Aikenhead's question had been left
unanswered. She was still convinced that Batterday had been
murdered to revenge one of his earlier victims, so why had no
other cases of his complaint been reported?

'Excuse me, madam.' The door had opened and she turned
and saw the tall figure of their housekeeper. 'Mr Raven has called
and would like to have a word with you.'

'Has he indeed?' Tania remembered their telephone conversation. Like the others the vicar had pre-judged Mark and she was
damned if she'd have anything to do with him. 'Tell Mr Raven I
am not at home, Mary.'

'If you wish, madam, but I think you should see him.' Mrs
MacDoggart was one of Raven's flock and very fond of him. 'The
poor gentleman's in some distress, and it would be a cruel thing
to send him away.'

'And so he should feel distressed.' Tania was about to flare at
her, and then relented. Raven was an old man who suffered from
ill health and his wife had recently had a nervous breakdown and
been sent to a mental institution. 'Oh, very well, show him in
here, Mary.'

'Lady Levin, will you ever be able to pardon me?' The Reverend James Raven had been a polio victim and he shuffled into the
room with a crab-like gait. 'I was told that Sir Marcus has been
home and obviously that means he is no longer suspected of the
attack on that poor child. But it also means that I have been guilty
of a terrible sin and I beg your forgiveness.'

'There's nothing to forgive, Vicar.' Tania took the outstretched
hand which was dry and cold and twisted by his complaint. 'We
all jump to wrong conclusions at times, so let's try to forget the
whole wretched business.'

'You are very kind – very charitable, but it will be a long
time before I can forgive myself. To think that I, a priest, could
condemn an innocent man out of spite and envy.

'Yes, envy is my cardinal sin, Lady Levin.' He looked around
the big, luxurious room with its regency furniture, rich leather

bindings in the shelves and sweeping views of the Thames. 'I was very ambitious in my youth. I dreamed of high office in the church. I wanted children and a wife people would admire. I also wanted money. As you must know I failed in every respect. No preferment; St Jude's is not even my own living, but a daughter church of Holy Innocents, and I am a priest-in-charge; a glorified curate. No children, and my dear Elizabeth will probably spend the rest of her life in an asylum. Where money is concerned, the proverbial church mouse is an apt description.' He gave the ghost of a smile. 'Subconsciously I must have begrudged your husband his success in life, and in my youth I had an experience which left me with a morbid horror of any form of sexual violence. So when I heard the rumours about Sir Marcus the tempter found me an easy prey.'

'The tempter.' Tania frowned as she motioned him to take a seat. Raven might be old and doddering; people said that his brain was failing and he would have to retire soon, but she had heard that he had once been a theological scholar of note. 'You believe that a personal devil exists, Vicar?'

'*Believe* is putting it too mildly.' He lowered himself stiffly into a chair. 'To some liberal members of my cloth, the *supernatural* has recently become a dirty word, but I know that Satan exists . . . that he never rests and his evil presence is always waiting in the shadows. Once I actually saw him face to face, Lady Levin.'

'The face of Satan.' Tania crossed to a cabinet and poured out two glasses of sherry. Raven's mental powers might be on the wane, but this was the kind of subject which interested her and Batterday's pictures crossed her mind. Also, the entwined numerals on a shroud and a T-shaped brand on a girl's forehead. 'What did he look like, Mr Raven?'

'Thank you, my dear.' He took a glass from her and stared down at the amber liquid as if seeing an image floating on its surface. 'The face of our enemy was entirely human and there was nothing outwardly sinister about him; no horns or goatish beard, or anything of that sort. But there was no nobility either – no resemblance to the Miltonian concept of evil. Lucifer, the Star of the Morning; a prince among the angels, who fell from grace.

'Just an ordinary man, on the surface, but behind quite commonplace features I sensed something foul; the bitterness of defeat, and there's no emotion fouler than that. Imagine a person destroying a work of art because he begrudges its maker's creative gift. Think of someone who suffers from an incurable illness and has lost all ambition except a burning desire to pass on his complaint to others. Both sins against the Holy Ghost, my dear. That is what I saw in the face of Satan.'

'When did this happen?' He had fallen silent and Tania prompted him. 'Please tell me.'

'A long time ago, my dear. I was presumptuous in those days . . . I thought I should understand the exact nature of the force my profession is ordained to fight and I happened to meet a man who was truly evil. I persuaded him that I had lost my faith and shared his beliefs that God is impotent and Satan rules the universe and he introduced me to a coven; a group of self-styled witches. One day they allowed me to be present at a ceremony.' The vicar was obviously troubled by the memory and he spoke with his head slumped towards his chest.

'The room was got up like a chapel and every object and ornament was designed to ridicule the Catholic mass. The cross had no headpiece and hung upside down from the ceiling, the candles were black and the censer stank of sulphur. The chalice contained excrement. Everything was wrong in some way or the other, but I, in my foolishness, did not take the performance seriously at first. The mockery was so blatant and inartistic that the whole ceremony was like a cheap theatrical performance intended to shock prudes. Right up to the end I thought that. Even the naked girl on the altar seemed to be an actress. Some harlot hired to take part in the obscene exhibition.' Raven raised his head and Tania saw that he was weeping.

'But when – when the priest climbed up on the altar – when he bent over the girl and she started to struggle, I realized the truth. It was no act – there was a real gag in her mouth – her legs really were held apart by a steel bar. She was not a prostitute or an actress, but a virgin and she was being deflowered by force. But I . . . I, Lady Levin, who believed I loved my God, did nothing.' The vicar pulled out a grimy handkerchief and wiped his streaming eyes. 'I saw him, you see. He had come into the room, he was looking at me, and when I tried to get up from my knees and tear that brute from the child's body, I just could not move. It was as if my own limbs were fettered and I'll never forget how he smiled. Such a mean little smile; a grin you might say, but it caused me actual physical pain . . . his eyes were like needles boring into mine.'

'Please go on, Vicar. What happened afterwards?' Raven had broken off, his chin was slumped even lower and Tania prompted him once more. She was amazed at the admission, because it appeared that he might have been involved in murder as well as witchcraft. 'Was the girl killed after the ritual?'

'Oh no. That would have invalidated everything and made the ceremony meaningless. She had become a chalice, a vessel of Satanic grace and her life had to continue. I believe that she was blindfolded and released somewhere near her home.' He sipped at his sherry and stood up. 'There was no chance that she might identify any of us. Apart from the priest, who came from another part of the country, we wore masks.

'That was the day when I discovered the existence of Satan, my dear . . . when I realized that the Wild Hunt is forever at our heels and evil is always on hand to tempt and destroy us.' The old man limped across to a window and frowned at the darkening sky. 'I think that experience tainted my soul and still does. After I left the chapel with its stench of sulphur and sweat and corruption the memory of those eyes remained with me and I was too frightened to contact the police.'

The Wild Hunt? Herbert Henson had mentioned that, Tania remembered. He had been speaking to John Batterday when he used the term and he had stressed the words harshly. 'But Mr Raven, surely the Wild Hunt is not led by Satan, but a being called Herne?'

'Satan inhabits the souls of his chosen servants, and Herne once served him well. And Herne has so many hunting grounds, hasn't he? His usual haunts are the Black Forest and the Forest of Fontainebleau, Windsor Great Park and the Welsh mountains, where he does not follow dogs but geese, the Gabriel Hounds, but he has many others and many other names, as I'm sure you know. We call him Herne, to the French he is Salathiel, to the

Germans, Hubert. But the creature is also Cartaphilus; Johannes Buttadaeus, the Undying One.'

'What . . . what did you say?' He had used the same guttural pronunciation as Henson had done in Batterday's house and Tania was on her feet and staring at him in amazement. 'The Undying One . . . Johannes who?'

'Buttadaeus – the door-keeper, of course.' Raven turned from the window and she saw that his distress had changed to academic interest. It was also clear that the subject engrossed him and he imagined she shared his knowledge. 'The word is dog Latin, of course . . . medieval, monastery Latin from around the thirteenth century, judging by the spelling *daeus* in place of *deus*.'

'But what does the name mean, Mr Raven?' The telephone was ringing, but Tania was oblivious to everything except her question. 'What is the English translation?'

'Surely that's obvious when one considers the story, Lady Levin?' He seemed disappointed by her ignorance. 'After all, Johannes Buttadaeus was the man who did *buffet* or *batter* God.'

Fourteen

'You have told us everything, Sir Marcus? We can answer any question put to us; but only if the data supplied by you is complete.' In his youth Mr Alexander England had wanted to practise law and he spoke like a barrister confronting a truculent client. 'Accurate and exact data, too. We allow no margins for error, and only work on facts.'

'I have provided you with all the information that is available.' Mark looked around the room which was windowless and completely air-conditioned. Fluorescent lamps glowed bleakly from the ceiling, the walls were coated with anti-condensation paint, though the atmosphere was arid, and the glaring red letters of an electric sign sternly prohibited smoking. In the centre of the floor stood a steel table around which five girls were bent over a battery of machines resembling outsized typewriters. The machines made a *zur-zur-zurring* noise as they spewed out the seventy-row punch-cards and the hum of suction tubes removing dust and chads from the apparatus had a distinctly hypnotic effect. The sounds and the monotony of their work had given the operators dazed expressions and they made Mark think of acolytes taking part in some repetitive religious ritual.

'The body had been partially consumed by pigs, Mr England, and the pituitary gland, the organ I really needed to examine, was missing. However, I think the rest of the medical data is comprehensive.' It was six hours since the corpse had been brought to Central Laboratories, and Mark and Paul Johnston had confirmed many of their earlier beliefs. John Batterday – Mark had no doubts that he was the man in question – had raped and infected Elsie Kerr. A sperm test had made that clear and his sweat glands contained traces of the same spores as hers had done. But he had not been an immune carrier in the true sense of the term. The organisms he had released were not germs or parasites, but intrinsic units of his own bodily system. They had not harmed him in any way at all: quite the opposite. Before death Batterday had been in perfect physical condition. The things were defence cells, but they had a structure and behaviour pattern quite unknown to earthly science.

So how had they developed and where had they and their host come from? Had a new strain of microscopic life been born on the planet, or was the outer space theory feasible? Possibly, but highly unlikely, because in every other way the man had been a normal human being. Mark was completely at a loss and he had come to England in desperation.

'Comprehensive perhaps, but I wish we'd had more time to make the information exhaustive.' England seemed unaware of the gravity of the situation, though Lord Aikenhead's statement had borne fruit too well. A voyeur had been lynched outside a public lavatory, several perfectly respectable men had been reported as rapists, and hospitals and surgeries were crammed with people demanding treatment for mysterious maladies. A further statement had announced that Elsie Kerr's attacker was dead, but that satisfied nobody; least of all Mark.

John Batterday had been murdered, his naked body had been fed to pigs, but before he died he had pulled off his gloves and struck a blow. Behind the corpse's right index fingernail Paul

Johnston had found a shred of skin. Thick calloused skin which could hardly have belonged to a female librarian. The nail had scratched somebody accustomed to heavy manual labour, and if it had penetrated the bloodstream that someone would be feeling very ill by now.

'Well, we shall examine the facts for you, Sir Marcus, but ours is not the brain of a seer or a gambler. We have no intuition; only a cold, dispassionate intelligence programmed to distinguish truth from falsehood. To discard everything that is not pertinent and base our findings on what remains.' Mr England was a lordly man and it almost sounded as if he were applying the royal 'we' to himself. He regarded his role as sacerdotal rather than regal, however, and shared Mark's thought that the punch-card operators resembled acolytes. In England's imagination the room was a temple and he was its high priest. The machines were prayer wheels and clanking censers, the no-smoking sign was an altar lamp showing that the sacrament was reserved, while against the wall stood the Holy of Holies – the House of God: a drab metal box that looked less impressive than an ordinary radio set.

But the interior of the box was impressive enough and it contained more electronic hardware than several hundred conventional radio receivers. England's god was a Smith-Lansberg ultra-micro-miniaturized computer and at the moment its integrated circuits were working on Mark's problem at the speed of light.

'If only the human factors were more efficient.' England glanced disdainfully at the table. Three of the girls had finished transcribing their data, and a male assistant had fed the perforated cards into the computer. But the other two operators were still at work and a dial on the box registered demands for more information.

'Now who can that be?' Any loud noise could disturb the computer's functioning and a flashing green light summoned England to the telephone. 'No, no, we can't possibly be disturbed at this juncture. Write down what she has to say and give it to Sir Marcus later.

'Your wife is on the line, but they'll make a note of her message.' He hung up and returned to Mark and Johnston, giving another irritated glance as he passed the table. The fourth girl had completed her transcriptions, she was drooping listlessly in her seat, and her partner had only a few more cards left. 'Lady Levin said she had some interesting news for you, but it can't be as important as this, eh?'

'I hope not.' Mark had felt only slight irritation at the peremptory attitude. He would have liked to know why Tania had rung, but he could hardly wait to hear the computer's announcement. England and his staff had been given every scrap of information he could think of, and not only the medical details. All that was known about John Batterday and Elsie Kerr was there for the oracle's inspection and soon it might deliver a verdict. The last girl had finished, her cards were being slipped into a slot at the side of the computer and a spool was winding out a strip of tape from its base.

'That is that, Sir Marcus. Our deliberations are complete, the sheep have been separated from the goats and, providing your data is sufficiently thorough, you will receive an answer.'

'You may go, ladies, and I won't need you either, Mr Hedges.' The spool was full and England carried it across to another apparatus, a bigger and outwardly more imposing machine than the computer with rows of dials and glowing lights. 'We must now wait for a translation.

'Do smoke if you wish, gentlemen.' The sign had gone out and England lit a cigarette while his assistants filed from the room, the man leading the way, and the girls following him as listlessly as sleep-walkers. 'When we are at work the prohibition is very necessary. Some of our circuits are so sensitive that the slightest change in atmosphere and temperature can affect them. As you doubtless know, Sir Marcus, the mean particle of tobacco smoke is as high as 0.6 microns.'

'I'm not a physicist, Mr England, and electronics are hardly my province.' Mark spoke coldly. He needed England's help – the computer was the most modern and sophisticated in London – but the man's condescension was infuriating. 'How long will the translation take?'

'We are now ready to deliver our findings.' It was the machine that answered him, but the voice issuing from its loudspeaker was just as lordly as England's. 'These findings are inconclusive for the following reasons.

'The data which has been presented to us is incomplete. The presentation of that data is inaccurate, incompetent and inexact.' England had turned up the volume and the domineering tones boomed loudly around the room. 'As an example of this incompetence let us first consider the attempted disposal of the corpse. It is quite untrue to suggest that the victim's flesh had been consumed by pigs.'

'That's a damned lie.' Paul Johnston had resented the charge of incompetence and he broke in angrily. 'I distinctly saw teeth marks, so what's the thing think it's up to?'

'The damage to the rib cage, base of skull and other bone structures took place while subject was alive and were caused by an axe, hatchet or similar instrument.' The machine drowned Johnston's protest. 'The pigs did not touch the body for two possible reasons. Either inborn warning devices lost to humanity informed them they were in the presence of danger or the clamour of the Gabriel Hounds frightened them into inactivity.' There was a pause and the three men looked at each other in bewilderment, because the term was unknown to all of them.

'We will now discuss the source of Miss Kerr's illness. This is an alien antibody, which produced severe glandular disturbances and early senility when transmitted to a third party. In its natural environment, however, this defence mechanism would render the original host virtually free from infection and cause rapid blood clotting should he be wounded.

'I naturally use the adjective *alien* in its meaning of exceptional. Only a fanciful and most ill-informed person could seriously consider an extra-terrestrial source.' It was Mark's turn to feel offended, though he was relieved to hear his theory was untrue. At the same time the computer had made one glaring error. There were definite teeth marks to show that the body had been savaged by the pigs.

'The man's longevity was probably due to glandular secretions, but without a report on the pituitary tissue it is impossible to say more than that. We suggest that the dental enamel be given extensive carbon-isotope tests.' Mark raised his eyebrows, because the machine was repeating nonsense. Elsie Kerr had died of a complaint that caused precocious senility, but the corpse had belonged to a man in his forties. Carbon-isotope tests were archaeological aids used to examine immensely old substances.

'Owing to the paucity of information, the cause of the subject's death is uncertain, but may have been due to the relaxation of a natural law.' Another nonsensical statement, Mark told himself, because the laws of nature cannot be broken, but the voice was adamant. 'Law in question is that relating to the Conservation of Energy as demonstrated by Huygens, Wallace and Wren in 1688.'

'But that's got nothing to do with biology or living matter.' It was England's turn to show surprise and he frowned deeply as the recording continued.

'Obviously the subject realized his potential danger to other human beings and took precautions to render himself harmless. This suggests that he was deeply repentant for his cardinal sin, and that the drug which prompted a sudden loss of sexual control was administered against his will; probably by the persons responsible for the destruction of his art collection. It is also probable that at least six of the mutilated pictures contained the subject's likeness.'

'Sorry, Sir Marcus.' The last suggestion was ludicrous and England had become much less lordly. 'The programming has slipped and we just can't help you. That happens at times because the mechanism is extremely sensitive – very temperamental indeed.' His frown deepened as the recording continued.

"Without confirmation by aforementioned carbon-isotope tests or further information we are unable to venture any more opinions, but suggest that the following sources should be referred to.'

'No, not yet.' England had been about to switch off the tape, but Mark shook his head because there might be something of value to be heard. Basically the computer was just a vast memory store and almost every fact known to man had been implanted in its circuits. They contained more information than a regiment of savants could absorb in their lifetimes, so what was he about to be told? What sources should he consult? Had some neglected men of science encountered the things that had turned Elsie Kerr old? Did an obscure medical journal describe a condition similar to John Batterday's?

'Refer to the writings of Beranger and Quintet.' The names were unfamiliar to Mark and he noted them in his diary. 'Study the work of Croly or its amplification by Lew Wallace, which was published in 1900 . . .' Obviously two more scientists who had escaped his attention and he cursed his ignorance while jotting them down. 'Consult the following . . .'

But Mark knew the last names well enough and he closed the diary in disgust when he heard them. England was right in thinking his bag of tricks was having an off day. However impressive its memory, the computer had lost selectivity and was producing random facts like a child delving into a bran tub. '. . . the novels of Eugene Sue and Caroline Norton . . . Also, "Queen Mab" and other poetical works by Percy Bysshe Shelley.'

Fifteen

'My wife gave you no idea when she'd be back? Thank you, Mary.' Mark replaced the telephone and looked at the note Tania had dictated for him. 'What's got into her, Brian? Tania's right back to her original nonsensical notion about ritual rape and black mass ceremonies. Read it yourself.'

'Thanks.' Plunket took the sheet of paper from him. They were at Mark's office at Central Laboratories and the dean had come over for news. Since Aikenhead's announcements the St Bede's switchboard had been jammed with inquiries and the hospital was in a virtual state of siege. Security guards were stationed at every entrance to ward off reporters and the morbidly curious, no patients were being admitted or discharged and only staff on urgent business were allowed to leave the premises.

'Tania has had a worrying time, Mark; we all have. Also, she's a Russian and they're extremely religious people. I was in Moscow attending a medical conference a couple of years back, and I saw the crowd filing through Lenin's tomb. Some of their expressions were quite extraordinary, and I'm damn sure half the women believed they weren't looking at an embalmed mummy, but a sleeping god.'

'But Tania's not like that. She may be imaginative, but she's level-headed enough; or was till she got friendly with Herbert Henson.' Mark's fingers drummed on the arm of his chair. 'And now she's gone off somewhere with our local vicar, another crackpot, who'll put more off-beat ideas into her head.'

'He'll have his work cut out to suggest anything more offbeat than this.' Plunket finished the note. 'She implies that this man Batterday had magical powers and was ritually sacrificed by people who hoped to deprive him of them for their own use. Magic indeed! The suspension of a natural law which every schoolboy knows is an impossibility.'

'Though probably Tania's views are no more absurd than my own were.' There was a crackle of fireworks and Mark looked towards the window and saw a rocket arching across the sky. November the fifth, he thought bitterly. Mankind might be in for a world-wide epidemic, but the tradition of maiming children, terrifying animals and destroying property had to be preserved. 'I mean the little green man from Mars, who provoked Aikenhead's scorn. Aikenhead was justified and Martians are dead and done with as far as I am concerned. Apart from those exceptional cell groups and glandular activity the body had no abnormality whatsoever. The man was as human as we are.

'This business is driving everyone round the bend. Everything too, Brian. I set great hopes on England's computer, but it flies off at a tangent and rambles about poets and novelists. It even denied the evidence of at least a dozen pairs of eyes. Every person who saw the corpse recognized teeth marks, yet according to the computer the pigs did not touch the flesh. Its view was that they instinctively recognized the toxic qualities or were frightened off by some phenomenon called the Gabriel Hounds.'

'That's not so far off-tangent.' The dean helped himself to more of Mark's whisky. 'There was a flock of geese around the paddock, I understand, and in Wales and the West Country wild geese are known as Gabriel's Hounds. Probably from the word *gabble*, and because the sound they make in flight resembles the baying of dogs following a scent.

'At least the computer has a poetic turn of phrase, Mark, and I gather you took one of its suggestions seriously. Johnston told me you're having the dental enamel subjected to carbon-isotope tests.'

'More fool I, probably, but as there's nothing to do but wait, we might as well keep the boffins busy.' Mark leaned far back in the chair and closed his eyes for a moment. 'I'm worried about Tania, Brian. However untenable her suggestions may be, Satanic cults do exist and some pretty unpleasant people belong to them. I don't like the idea of her and Raven playing amateur detectives one little bit.'

'Then why not get on the blower to that parson fellow and see just what she is doing, old boy?' The dean pushed the phone towards him but Mark shook his head.

'I tried to, Brian, but it's no good. Apparently he's not on the telephone. A strange thing for a priest, but there you are.'

'Then go and pay him a call in person. As you say, there's nothing for you to do here till . . .' He didn't bother to complete the sentence because the end was obvious. Elsie Kerr and John Batterday had provided little information. In one case Genomycin had destroyed the alien cells; in the other they had started to mortify with the rest of the body as soon as Batterday's heart stopped beating; also there had been no pituitary gland to examine.

But somewhere there might be a person who had only just begun to develop the symptoms of the illness, and if he or she was found soon enough . . . if a sliver of pituitary tissue could be removed immediately after death, the battle might be won. Cultures could be grown, the exact nature of the organism studied, and from those cultures a vaccine produced to curb further infection.

'I can't leave the building, Brian.' Mark's eyes were fixed on an intercom on his desk. 'At any second that contraption may report a genuine case and we can get busy.' He stressed the word *genuine* because public anxiety was at boiling point. Almost every ailment from tertiary syphilis to hangovers were being reported as 'Rampant Progeria', as the press described the condition, and Lord Aikenhead bitterly regretted making so flamboyant a statement. But Mark had no regrets. At least one person had received a scratch from Batterday's nails and at least two people – the man and the woman who had plied the farmer with drinks – had handled Batterday's naked body. He was quite sure that one of those persons must have been infected and the disease was about to reveal its full powers – to come into the open like an army with banners.

'Why don't they give themselves up and ask for help, Brian?' He watched another rocket soar over the rooftops. 'They may be murderers dreading arrest, but Aikenhead described the symptoms very vividly. They know what could happen if they don't get treatment and not even a lunatic would prefer that horror to a few years in prison.

'But just a moment.' He reached out for the note again. 'Both Tania and the computer considered that a law of nature may have been violated and though that seems nonsensical to us, is there a chance they could be right?' Mark hurried over to a shelf of reference books and pulled out his diary. England had admitted that the computer's programming had gone awry and the information it gave valueless. Because of that he had not bothered to obey its instructions, but he and England were fallible human beings.

'Refer to the writings of Beranger and Quintet . . . Study the work of Croly and its amplification by Lew Wallace . . .' That was what he had been told to do and at first he had imagined the machine was referring to scientists whose work was unfamiliar to him. But apparently *Who's Who in Medicine* shared his ignorance and he replaced the heavy volume.

All the same, he had time on his hands and there was no harm in making a check. He re-read Tania's note and pressed a switch on the intercom. 'Levin here, Mr England. Sorry to trouble you again, but I'd like to ask your bag of tricks a further question.'

'Tonight, Sir Marcus?' England sounded resentful. He had not liked the expression 'bag of tricks' and was still mortified by his oracle's failure. Also he had his coat on and was just preparing to go home. 'I'm afraid that's quite impossible. The circuits can't be reprogrammed till tomorrow, and even then we may be unable to help you. Your earlier data was most unsatisfactory.'

'This is a very simple question, Mr England, concerning a point the computer raised on its own accord. Please write down what I want answered.'

'I see.' England had noted the query, and though he obviously did not see at all, he became more cooperative. 'Well, we'll have a go, Sir Marcus, though I can't for the life of me imagine why you require the information. As I said, the names must be quite irrelevant to your problem. However, hold the line and I'll inquire what we have to say.'

'Just barking up trees again, Brian; probably quite the wrong ones.' Mark grinned at Plunket's bewilderment, but for some reason he was quite sure that the information could be vital. He was also completely confident that one of the people who had killed Batterday was already experiencing the symptoms of ill health, and the murderers made him think of rats. Diseased rats, plague rats; rats tortured by *bacillus pestis*, who remain underground till their agony becomes unbearable and then crawl out of the sewers to die and spread contagion.

'We are ready now, Sir Marcus.' England's voice returned to the intercom and a second or two later it was followed by the booming tones of the loudspeaker.

'You desire to know what the following have in common: Beranger – Croly – Norton – Shelley – Sue – Wallace.' The names thudded out like the blows of boxing gloves. 'The list is incomplete and at least three others should be included. Bishop Thomas Percy, Matthew Paris and the person using the pseudonym Cronus.

'With the exception of the last, these are all well-known literary figures and we would have imagined the connection would have been obvious to anyone with a modicum of education.' The apparatus appeared to be programmed to deliver insults as well as information and it paused to let the jibe sink in.

'Each of these writers was concerned with the mystery surrounding Johannes Buttadaeus ... Repeat, *Buttadaeus*, the Wandering Jew.'

'I think there should be a reference in this one too.' Raven had flicked through another musty volume. 'Yes, here we are, Lady

Levin. Page ninety-seven.' He had marked the place with a strip of newspaper and then looked at his watch. 'But, oh dear, duty calls, I see. Evensong, and I shall be late already. Will you excuse me? I hate to leave you, as the story interests me as much as it does you, but I really must go. Make yourself completely at home and I shall be back just as soon as I can.' He had hurried off and left Tania at work in the den, as he called his study.

And a very dirty den it was. Everything was disordered, dust lay everywhere; Tania's hands were grey from handling the books and now and then she heard a rustle of mice behind the wainscot. The vicarage was an exact opposite to John Batterday's spotless bungalow, but Raven certainly had a fine collection of works on theology and folklore and Tania was too engrossed to consider her surroundings.

'Worn by his sufferings, Our Lord did seek to rest by the door of the judgment hall.' She was reading from a translation of the Luneberg Abbey *Chronicle*. 'But Cartaphilus, the keeper of the gate, did spit upon Him and strike Him saying, "Go on faster, Jesus." Whereupon the Man of Sorrows replied, "I am going, but verily thou shalt tarry till I come again."'

Ahasuerus – Cartophilus – Lakedion – Salathiel ben Sadi – Johannes Buttadaeus. Five of the several names given to a person who had once done a very cruel and foolish thing and paid dearly for it. In some versions of the legend he had been the gate-keeper, in others a cobbler, in one a servant of Pontius Pilate. But they all agreed as to the nature of his sin and the punishment that followed.

'For this act, the Jew was condemned to wander the four corners of the earth till Christ's second coming.' Raven had marked passages in all the appropriate books and Tania turned to Bethune's *History of Western Mythology*. The man was first recognized at Antwerp during the thirteenth century and admitted that he had witnessed the Crucifixion. Other appearances took place at regular intervals during the years. At Prague in 1602, at Stamford forty-eight years later, at Venice in . . .' A dozen other place-names and dates followed and the most recent manifestation had been at Salt Lake City, scarcely more than a hundred years ago. 'In each case he was described as an ordinary human being, though tortured by guilt and craving to be released from his long life.

'But according to North European tradition this release is occasionally granted.' Tania frowned at the text. 'The Jew falls into a trance and when he awakes he loses his human form and becomes a supernatural and satanic figure; Herne, or Hubert, the Wild Huntsman, who rides through the forests of England, France and Germany, and it is death for a mortal man to look upon him. A Cornish and Welsh version of the legend states that the Hunter's pack does not consist of dogs, but wild geese which are known as the Gabriel Hounds, and this is supported by a legend common in Bavaria.' The next page showed a reproduction of a medieval woodcut and Tania's heartbeats quickened. The picture was not the same as the one she had seen on Batterday's wall, but the title and the subject matter were identical: a man surrounded by seven long-necked birds.

'*Die sieben Pfeifer.*' She read the title and the text beneath the illustration aloud. ' "In his human form Buttadaeus is sometimes accompanied by a flock of geese or swans known as the Seven Whistlers whose duty is to protect him from insult and physical violence." '

This would not do. Tania rapped a hand against her forehead. The facts were fitting together and every reference she came to suggested that her theory was correct. The birds, the similarity of names, a passport showing that John Batterday had been a constant wanderer, the pictures. Above all the pictures: if the police were right in thinking they were originals, Batterday must have purchased them from the actual artists, and Dürer died in 1528.

But the Wandering Jew was just a legend, a myth, and she had to stop her imagination running riot. Folk stories were for children and primitive people, they have no place in modern civilization. Also, if the phenomenon had a shred of truth, the story itself invalidated her suspicions about John Batterday. Johannes Buttadaeus had been doomed to walk the earth till Christ's second coming released him. But Batterday was dead all right. Mark had convinced her of that and she had seen his corpse.

If only she could discuss the subject with somebody rational. Not James Raven, who was eaten up with superstition and would believe anything. Somebody like Mark who could cynically demolish the ogre's castle she had erected in her mind. Better still a man such as Herbert Henson, who believed in the occult, but was essentially practical. Yes, Henson was the obvious confidant and she'd been very rude to him. It was he who had rung while she was talking to Raven – he'd wanted news of Mark and Elsie Kerr. She had told Mrs MacDoggart to say that she would call him back and then driven off to the vicarage with Raven, completely forgetting the promise.

If only she could speak to Henson now. Tania cursed the vicar's lack of a telephone and then opened the last book he had produced for her examination. A little octavo volume wrapped in brown paper as though its cover were erotic, and she had noticed that Raven had hesitated before pulling it from the shelf.

The Quest for the Wanderer. The title page showed that the book was a privately published work by someone using the pseudonym 'Cronus' and only fifty copies had been issued.

'The joint legends of the Jew and the Wild Hunter have fascinated me since childhood, and after endless study I became convinced that such a being has existed on this planet for almost two thousand years and still walks among us. A creature with two physical forms and two spiritual natures. Human, but immortal . . . at times a cringing penitent, at others a true servant of Lucifer. This conviction was reached from the following sources. The chronicles of Matthew Paris – Bishop Percy's Reliques – the *Flores Historium* by Roger of Wendover – Paulus von Fitzen's account of his meeting with the man in 1523 . . .' The whole of the opening page was devoted to references and Tania turned to the next. 'But my final conclusion was formed from a passage written by the twelfth-century French troubadour, Bertran de Bors.' The rustling from the skirting board had grown louder and Tania glanced sideways and saw a little grey shape emerge from a hole and scamper across the floor.

'Our Saviour did make unto the evil doer one promise. "As my blood and my body do bring grace to those who follow me, thine shall contaminate and corrupt. But peace will be granted when thou art forced to sin unwillingly and are by men more evil than thyself consumed." '

Impossible or not – fantasy, myth, fairy story, the quotation seemed to have solved the main problem. If the author of the little book was not an impostor or a cranky fraud who had invented references to support his case . . . if his work had been read by people who were eager to accept the evidence . . . the kind of people who might brand a girl's forehead and dress a corpse in a ceremonial scarf, the puzzle was complete. Tania recalled the car moving away from the kerb, the sound of the shot and how she had swung round to see Henson kneeling over the body of a man who later claimed his wound was superficial. People like that were visionaries, but they were also cautious. Their first move would be to discover whether Batterday could be killed by conventional methods and that could be why the shot had been fired. Their next action would be to force him to sin again and turn a medieval belief into a twentieth-century menace.

Tania stood up quickly and reached for her handbag. Another mouse had left the hole, but she was not frightened of rodents. She was terrified of something else, however, and she had to talk to the book's author as soon as possible. With any luck that might not be difficult.

Cronus was the name of a deity; the father of Pluto, Lord of the Underworld. But it was also a name she had recently seen heading an article in Herbert Henson's *Psychic Observer*.

Sixteen

'The trouble is that the first symptoms of the illness are almost identical to the current influenza strain that's going the rounds.' Brian Plunket was studying a report that had just reached Mark's office. 'People are clamouring for treatment. Over five hundred suspected cases have been hospitalized in Greater London alone, but you can't admit everybody who complains of a mild attack of flu. Nor is the supply of antibiotics limitless. They're turning 'em away in thousands and one or two might just be genuine.

'But you're not listening to a word I'm saying, are you?' He frowned at Mark, who had been standing silently by the window for a full five minutes. 'You're still thinking about that computer and you'd better snap out of it, old boy. We're supposed to be scientists, not Congolese witch-doctors, and the message was meaningless, because the wretched machine was incorrectly programmed. What if a number of writers did concern themselves with the same legend? The Wandering Jew is a mythological figure who never existed, so do try and be logical.'

'I'm trying very hard to be, Brian, but reason and logic don't seem to apply at the moment, and how can we be sure the man did not exist?' Mark turned from the window and walked slowly back to his desk. 'We know that Batterday had an abnormally strong resistance to infection. We know that his blood might have clotted with extreme rapidity – an opposite condition to haemophilia, which would have closed a wound as effectively as stitches. We suspect that his pituitary produced hormone secretions capable of slowing the ageing process.'

'I'm not denying that, Mark.' Plunket's pipe rapped the desk sharply. 'Certain diseases, such as the Parkinson syndrome which steadies the heart function, do tend to prolong life, but not to any appreciable extent, and what you're suggesting is quite untenable. I was prepared to accept an outer space origin, but this present line of reasoning is both ludicrous and morbid. It goes against the universal laws which cannot be broken.'

'How do we know they're unbreakable, Brian? We're so short-lived – humanity's been such a short time on this planet – what do we really know about anything?' Mark sat down and stretched out his legs beneath the desk. 'Imagine an insect stationed outside St Bede's. For five days it sees you arrive each morning and leave at night, and believes your routine is constant: an unbreakable, natural law.

'But on the sixth day, Saturday, when you don't come to the hospital the poor, short-lived brute is dead and it never knew that the law was a fallacy.'

'Hardly a valid analogy, old boy.' The dean rammed tobacco into his pipe. 'Archimedes and Newton and Pythagoras were not insects.'

'No, they were apes like you and me, Brian.' Mark watched Plunket light the pipe; grey smoke drifting to the ceiling and dispersing like memories of past events fading from the mind. 'We are primitive creatures, only just down from the trees, and what do we know about creation? If there is an all-powerful God He could suspend as many laws as He liked. After all, He made them.

'This might be what we're waiting for, Brian.' His hand shot out as the telephone rang, but he picked it up very slowly. The message would give him the data he needed. One human being was a necessary price to halt disaster, but what if several cases had been confirmed simultaneously and the epidemic had started? 'Levin here.'

'Sir Marcus, I know you are only accepting official calls, but I have a Mr James Raven on the line.' The operator was clearly nervous at interrupting him. 'Mr Raven says his business concerns your wife and it is vital that he is put through to you.'

'I'll talk to him.' Raven was an unexpected caller, but a very welcome one. 'Good evening, Vicar. Is Tania with you?'

'I'm afraid not, Sir Marcus, and I'm worried about her – extremely worried.' Raven had run to the telephone booth and his breath came in gasps. 'Your wife came over to the vicarage because she wished to consult certain of my books on folklore and I left her there when I went to take Evensong.

'But when I got back I found a note from her on my desk. Do you know a man named Henson – Professor Herbert Henson?'

'I do indeed, Vicar.' Mark's personal anxieties were on the boil again and he thought of something which had not seemed significant when he first heard it. Tania and Henson had been with John Batterday when the shot was fired at him. Why should anybody attempt to kill or maim a man in the presence of witnesses? 'What about Henson, Mr Raven?'

'I gather that you wife is on her way to see him and this is what worries me. I know nothing about Henson, but the note states that she is hoping he will put her in touch with a person who writes under the name of "Cronus" and him I do know. I know how he can influence and corrupt people, and if your wife falls under his spell as I once did . . .' The time pips sounded and there was a pause as Raven rummaged for change and a coin rattled in the box. 'Sir Marcus, the man calling himself Cronus is a defrocked Jesuit priest named Cedric Hamilton and he is without doubt the most wicked human being I have ever encountered.'

*

'For he's a jolly good driver, and so say all of us . . . and so say all of us . . . For he's a jolly good driver . . .'

'Noisy little bleeders.' The children's enthusiasm was quite genuine but Sidney Rutter did not appreciate the compliment and he scowled while manoeuvring the school bus through the evening traffic. The kids were naturally excited. This was Guy Fawkes' night and they were on their way to a firework display. But there was no need to make such a racket, and why the hell didn't the teachers stop them? He glanced through the driving mirror at three women seated in the rear of the coach. They looked almost as eager as their charges and obviously hadn't got his imagination – they couldn't visualize what might happen to them in the near future.

THIS IS THE MAN. Rutter slowed at an intersection and once more the enlargement of a passport photograph stared at him through the windscreen, DO YOU KNOW HIM – HAVE YOU TOUCHED HIM? – DID YOU KILL HIM? That was the third news-stand he had passed since picking up the children and there seemed to be nothing else in the evening papers. THE LUCIFER GERM – RAMPANT PROGERIA – APPEAL TO KILLERS.

'For he's a jolly good driver, and so say all of us.' He wanted to listen to the coach radio, but it was impossible with those brats yelling themselves hoarse, though he'd heard enough to realize how serious things were. 'At this stage there is no need for the general public to be alarmed, but it is essential that the persons responsible for the death of John Batterday receive treatment.' A note of passion had crept into the announcer's voice. 'It is to those people I am appealing and whoever you are – whatever your motives, I warn you that further delay may be fatal. You are probably infected by a hideous disease, and you must report to the nearest hospital immediately.'

Like hell they'd report. They were murderers, weren't they? Cold-blooded killers, who probably believed the announcements were lies; a trick by the police to lure them into captivity. They could be right, too, because the symptoms described in the first statement had been too horrible and repulsive to be taken seriously and they hadn't been repeated since. Sidney Rutter tried to reassure himself, but he knew he was wrong and his thoughts kept returning to his own physical condition. He'd felt fit enough till an hour or two ago, but he was tired now: really tired. Maybe it was just overwork – he'd been putting in a lot of extra hours to save the deposit for the house Madge demanded before she'd marry him – or else he might be starting a cold. But suppose it wasn't overwork or a cold ... suppose that ... He concentrated on passing a crawling taxi, but his fears returned as soon as it was behind him.

Growing old overnight – breathing and heartbeats weakening – teeth loosening in the gums – hair becoming grey – the skin wrinkling. Somewhere in London or the Home Counties there were people who had handled a diseased body. People who had probably caught the disease and could spread it to others. People who would not give themselves up because they disbelieved the warnings, or were more frightened of the law than ill health.

People who could pass on the complaint to others. To those kids, so excited at the thought of the fireworks; to their cheerful-looking teachers who should have cancelled the outing when the whole of London was menaced; to himself. Another line of placards slid past to increase his anxiety: THE SATAN GERM – PRECOCIOUS OLD AGE.

Tiredness would probably be the first sign of infection and out of the back of his mind Rutter remembered a quotation which described the last symptoms, '... mere oblivion; sans teeth, sans eyes, sans taste, sans ...' He couldn't remember the final word, he'd been about the same age as the children when he'd been made to learn it, and to hell with the kids and their teachers. What might happen to him? To Sidney Rutter, who kept himself in good shape – a daily run in the park wet or shine, and never a serious illness in his life. Who didn't smoke or drink and whose only vice was an odd tumble with Madge in the back of the car. '... sans *everything*.' That was the missing word, of course, and it described just what the disease could do to you. Blind, deaf, toothless and completely without feeling in a few hours, and then there'd be the void, nothing at all.

Like hell there'd be nothing. Rutter used the blasphemy a third time because it was his favourite expression, which often gave him reassurance by mocking his inner fears. But a scarlet neon sign glowing in the sky reminded him of his youth and he shuddered at the memory of his foster father reading aloud from one of the early Christian philosophers. 'In that lowest circle of hell the damned lie so tightly packed together that a hand cannot be lifted to remove from the eye the worm that gnaws it.'

Rutter was an orphan who'd been adopted into a family of fanatical Calvinists, and though he claimed to have rejected their teachings, he knew he lied. He was not a hypochondriac because he feared sickness, but because death itself terrified him. Reason might assure him that no god would torture a creature he had made in his own image, but Rutter's instinct knew better. Satan did exist, there was a hell, and the people who had killed a man named Batterday had unlocked its doors. At any moment the hour might strike and then . . . 'sans taste, sans everything'.

He recited aloud, but the children's voices drowned the verse. Happy, excited children on their way to a party – to a firework night. Children who were paying Sidney Rutter homage with their own verses. 'For he's a jolly good driver, and so say all of us.'

'The most wicked man I have ever encountered.' Raven had told him a great deal before he ran out of change and they were cut off, and the sentence kept running through Mark's mind while he looked up Henson's number.

Cedric Hamilton, a defrocked priest who used the *nom de plume* 'Cronus', had written a monograph claiming that the Wandering Jew story was factual. Hamilton had once introduced Raven to a group of perverted devil worshippers. Hamilton was a subscriber to a magazine edited by Herbert Henson. Tania was hoping Henson would introduce her to him and she had to be stopped. Because if Tania's earlier suspicions were correct – if Satanism was responsible for Batterday's death – Canon Hamilton might have acquaintances who would be feeling very sorry for themselves. The occupants of a car who had fired at a man to see whether conventional weapons could harm him. A middle-aged couple who had made a farmer drunk to ensure that his pigs went hungry. The people who had wrapped a naked body in a shroud. Mark had found the number, but he had difficulty in dialling it because his eyes suddenly blurred and he saw a ravaged face interposed above the numerals. Elsie Kerr's face – any girl's face – perhaps Tania's face, growing old and wrinkled.

'The results of the carbon-isotope tests, sir.' The door had opened and Paul Johnston hurried into the room. He had a sheet of photostat in his hand and seemed puzzled. 'I can't make head nor tail of them.'

'Tell me later, Paul.' Johnston had held out the paper, but Mark waved him aside. Henson's number was ringing and soon he would be able to contact Tania. He had to stop her, and if he failed John Batterday would have claimed another victim.

'I don't know what this means, Doctor, but everything seems to be going haywire today.' Johnston was showing the report to Plunket. 'Dental enamel is a stable substance, not subject to decay, and three specimens were tested. Yet each result was the same. It just doesn't make sense.'

'Eight – eight – two – four – six – eight—' The phone had been lifted, but before the voice finished repeating the number Mark rang off, dropping his own instrument into the rest as though its plastic cover were red hot. Either there was a fault on the line or the owner of the voice was suffering from a heavy cold. The words had sounded thick and distorted and they reminded him of something Tania had mentioned quite casually. A scrap of seemingly trivial information, but it suggested that one of her extravagant theories was true. Henson had kept giving Batterday's name a guttural pronunciation, as if stressing the possibility that it was based on a foreign original.

'I haven't a car with me, Paul, and I need one badly.' He held out his hand. 'May I have the keys of your Mini, please?'

'Of course, sir. It's parked in the usual space. But don't you want to see these results?' The young man's bewilderment increased. 'They must be wrong, yet the tests are supposed to be infallible.'

'All I want is a car, so please give me the keys.' Mark snatched them from him and then underlined an entry in the phone book. 'I've no time to explain, but get through to Scotland Yard and tell Commander Trant to go to this address as soon as possible. And I want you to rustle up a decontamination squad, Brian, and send it there.'

Mark strode out of the room and he broke into a run when he reached the corridor. It was cavalierish to keep Johnston and Plunket in ignorance, but he really had no time to waste. In fact he might be too late already. He knew why Henson had given Batterday's name a guttural note. Henson suspected who Batterday was and had tried to provoke him into an admission.

Mark could also guess what the isotope tests had revealed. Mr John Batterday had been born in the same century as Jesus Christ.

Seventeen

'Away with you, Jesus. Go on faster ... faster ... faster.' Tania considered the story while she drove through the thinning late-evening traffic. The most common version stated that the words had been accompanied by a blow to the face, another by a kick, a third by a gob of spittle. But whatever had occurred, it produced a terrible reply. 'I am going, but verily thou shalt tarry till I come again.'

So, Ahasuerus or Cartophilus – one of those had probably been his original name – had gone out on the long journey, and over the centuries his nature had split into several forms and other names had been given him. Buttadaeus, the man who struck God and was deeply repentant for the crime. Salathiel, the mysterious sixteenth-century Venetian. Lakedion, the Undying One who craved death.

Those were the Wanderer's innocent guises, but from time to time he returned to the service of Satan, his former master, the horn sounded in the forests of Bavaria and Fontainebleau and Windsor, Herne followed his Gabriel Hounds over the Western hills, and men died or lost their sanity at his approach.

'The Larches' – Thames Reach. Tania had never been to Herbert Henson's house, but she had checked the directions on the car map and it couldn't be far off. She had passed the park and the landing-stage for pleasure steamers, and big Victorian mansions loomed around her. Imposing, four-storied villas, built for bankers and merchants, which had fallen on evil times when the electric railways came and their owners moved out to the country. Till a few years ago they had been slums, but now the district was fashionable again, and very sought-after by the cultivated rich. Actors and television personalities, barristers and publishers and film producers had lavished money on the old houses and most of them were as spruce as Batterday's bungalow. The street lights showed up fresh paint and pastel stucco, and carriage lamps proclaimed a welcome in most of the porches.

'. . . tarry till I come again,' she thought. A bitter sentence to inflict. Age had not touched Buttadaeus – no illness or wound had given him peace – shipwreck and snowstorm and probably hundreds of other disasters that had killed his companions had left him unscathed. He had been forced to live on through the generations, and to a sane human being that would be the worst punishment of all.

But would everyone think so? Were there people who had sold themselves to evil and craved longevity because they dreaded hellfire? People who understood the darker side of the Wanderer's nature and envied the powers that went with them? The kind of people she hoped Herbert Henson might lead her to.

Tania slowed to read a street sign and turned right. This was Thames Reach at last and, providing Henson was at home, she should soon know who Cronus was. The professor must have the names and addresses of the *Psychic Observer's* subscribers and if he didn't keep copies of them at his private residence she'd make him take her to the magazine's office and go through the files. After that, a telephone call would send the police on the trail of Batterday's murderers.

Because the man who called himself Cronus had provided an explanation of how an immortal being could die. 'But peace will be granted when thou art forced to commit a sin unwillingly and art by men more evil than thyself consumed.'

Cronus had also provided Tania with a great deal of information about himself. The little book had been limited to fifty copies, which meant that it was only intended for friends and associates, one of whom must have been James Raven, and Cronus had written the following passage: 'Some day, the whereabouts of the man will be revealed to me and when that happens the star of the sky will guide our hand.' *Star* – not *stars*, was the significant point. Cronus had not referred to any astral body, but to Lucifer, the Star fallen from Heaven, the greatest of the archangels. Tania was quite certain that Cronus was the person who had once introduced Raven to a witches' coven, she was sure that the coven still existed and its meeting place was her journey's end.

And this was the end of the present journey. The street was cluttered with parked cars and she pulled into the first available space and set off on foot. 'The Larches' was the last house in the road and easily recognizable by three tall trees dominating a garden which sloped down to the river's edge, where a motorboat was moored. It was bigger than its neighbours and the architect had been a man with grandiose notions. The steeply gabled roof was surrounded by mock battlements and four gothic towers stood at its corners. They looked lowering and sinister against the night sky, but suddenly the effect was altered by a cluster of fireworks that burst directly overhead and bathed the building in silver light.

No light came from the house itself, though. The door and all the visible windows were in complete darkness, and Tania cursed herself for not telephoning from a public call-box to see if Henson was at home.

But it was all right. As Tania crossed the street she saw that four cars were parked in the drive – Henson's 3-litre Rover, a Jaguar and two battered Fords. Herbert was at home, but he had visitors, which was a nuisance. She must get him on his own and talk privately. And if the information regarding Cronus was at the magazine office she'd have to persuade him to leave his guests, which might be difficult.

'Oh, hurry up and answer.' She had rung three times, but there was no reply. The cars suggested that the house was occupied, but the building itself had an atmosphere of complete deadness. She rang again and stood watching a tug dragging three heavily-laden barges up the river. The boat was struggling against the tide and its thudding diesels drowned a distant crackle of fireworks. Probably they also drowned the bell, and when the convoy passed somebody would hear her.

The catch was not fastened. She had given the bellpush a vicious jab and the door swung open to reveal a dimly lit hall.

Tania stepped inside and raised her voice. 'Is anyone at home? It's Tania Levin, Professor.'

There was no reaction, but there were people in the house. From a passage facing her there came a low murmur of voices and Tania walked towards it, calling out again as she did so. 'Professor Henson, are you there?'

They must have heard her now. She could make out individual voices. A woman who sounded hysterical and a man with a heavy cold. Tania walked on and then paused. The sounds were drifting up from a staircase at the end of the corridor and with them came a smell. A mixture of odours which was spicy and chemical and also animal; a sickly, cloying tang that she felt she should recognize.

'Help – help – help.' The woman was repeating the word, but not as a cry for assistance. It sounded as if she were pleading forgiveness. 'We have failed and we must find help from someone.'

'We are past human help, my dear.' That was Henson's voice, but there was nothing fruity or pompous about it. He wheezed and spluttered as though phlegm were choking him. 'We have sinned because we were deluded by a false prophet and our only hope is that the impostor's sacrifice will be accepted and He will pardon and heal us.'

'Let us go down on our knees and see how we erred.' The next speaker was a man with a Cockney accent. 'Let Him show us how the sacred vessel of His wrath was broken. Let Him tell us what we must do to be pardoned.'

There was a shuffling and a creak of furniture and Tania's flesh crawled. She knew that she had reached journey's end – knew who the voices belonged to. She also knew that there was only one sensible thing for her to do. Turn, creep out of the house and run for her life. But she didn't turn – her curiosity was so great that she couldn't even remain where she was and, as if cords were tugging at her feet, she moved on down the stairs towards the half-open door that lay beyond them.

'Heal us, Lord – accept the sacrifice we have made for Thee – make us clean again for we have done to him what was done to Thine enemy.' Several voices were speaking in unison and the smell grew stronger and stronger as Tania approached the door.

She had recognized two of its elements: one was incense and the other burning sulphur. But the third still escaped her. A sickly, sour odour that made her want to vomit.

'Show us how we erred, Great One.' The lights beyond the doorway dimmed and were replaced by a single square of colour, and Tania halted. She could see into the room now, and though the lighting made the view shadowy and indistinct it was clearly a chapel, and some three dozen people were on their knees before an altar. On one side of the altar a vast marble image was stationed, on the other a man. An equally large man dressed in a cassock who held his arms outstretched and stood as rigidly as his stone companion.

But though the scene was eerie enough, it was the coloured square above the altar that made Tania choke back a cry of astonishment. She was looking at a film, and the actress on the screen was herself. A recently painted front door had opened and she had walked out on to a porch, smiled at John Batterday and moved off down a path.

Batterday and Henson were in camera now, Henson bidding their host a formal goodbye, and then raising his left hand to someone or something off screen. Henson smiling slightly at Batterday's face as its mouth shot open. Henson nodding complacently as Batterday's body crumpled on to the steps.

The scene changed, and the next sequence had been filmed from the interior of a car that was driving very slowly along a dimly lit street. The quality of the film was rather poor till the car stopped and the front-seat passenger, Herbert Henson, opened his door and beckoned to a little fair-haired girl who was waiting for a bus.

The attempt to kill Batterday – Elsie Kerr's abduction! The men and women kneeling before her were methodical people. They had recorded their progress pictorially and Tania was being shown every separate action. She saw three men enter Batterday's house, she saw fists beat him unconscious. She saw ink and knives and a cigar stub at work on his pictures. She saw a hypodermic syringe enter his vein.

'It must have been here – here that the ritual was wrongly performed, so pardon us. Master, and show us how to atone.' A voice croaked from one of the kneeling figures, and the following scene showed the actual room that housed them, and they were all present, though their faces were masked, as was the face of the priest and his two servers. The girl's was the only face uncovered, and though she was chained against the altar Tania could imagine her expression as the ceremonial scourge laced her back and the red hot brand marked her forehead.

But another actor had entered the set and there was no mask obscuring his features. Those very familiar features, which Tania hardly recognized because emotion seemed to have changed the whole structure of the face. The prophecy stated that the Wanderer would be granted release if he committed his final sin under compulsion and he was about to do so. The drug his captors had forced him to accept had blotted the human side of his nature and it was not a man Tania saw walking towards the altar, but a satyr. A creature from the pit whose expression made Dürer's and Bosch's studies of evil appear almost innocent. The horn had sounded and the Wild Huntsman was riding to hounds.

Tania couldn't look at him any more. The mad, satanic eyes were too much for her. She knew she would scream if she saw the climax of the ceremony and she turned her eyes away from the picture. As she did so the projector flickered off the screen for a second, something metallic glinted in its beam and she remembered a recently used phrase. 'We have done to him what was done to Thine enemy.'

It was then that Tania screamed and she never saw the lines of faces pivot towards her. She never heard the voice shouting her name, or the footsteps pounding down the stairs behind her. All her mind would register was that tall figure who stood rigidly stationed beside the altar.

No, not stationed – not standing – not yet rigid – not so very tall. Canon Hamilton, or Cronus, to use the pen-name, was paying for his error of judgment. His feet were off the floor and nails held him suspended from a wall.

'That's right, Peter Freake, make a nuisance of yourself . . . spoil the pleasure for everybody else as usual. Ouch!' Miss Barbara Yard, the second mistress of St Cuthbert's primary school, had rapped the bullet-head of one of her charges and instantly regretted the action.

'Are you going to behave or be sent back to the coach?' The firework display was designed to have educational and aesthetic value and though the majority of the audience were enjoying themselves, there was as always a dissenting element, and the organizers had taken few safety precautions. The fireworks were being let off from a landing-stage while over three hundred children from several schools were lined up along the towpath. The only barrier was a rope, and beyond it a line of steep steps led straight down to the river.

'I asked you a question, Peter.' Bullet-head looked quite unrepentant and she considered giving him another rap, but desisted, wishing she had a ruler handy. Freake by name and freak by nature was the only way to describe the beast. His skull really was rock-hard; certainly much harder than her knuckles, and the punishment had hurt her very much more than it had hurt him. 'Do you want to sit alone in the coach and miss the rest of the show?'

'No, Miss Yard, but I was only 'avin' a bit-er-fun, like.' The boy's eyes were glued on a battery of Roman candles. The bit of fun had been to jostle a small and inoffensive child through the barrier. He'd hoped to push him right down into the water, he knew old Barnyard realized his intention, but he was certain she wouldn't dare send him back to the bus. Left on his own he'd rip the seat cushions, that he would. 'But why ain't there no Guy, Miss, and when are the clowns comin'? Should 'ave a Guy and clowns at a party.'

'Guy – Clowns?' Miss Yard cursed her occupation. She had an honours degree in philosophy, a teaching diploma and she'd once written a highly-praised thesis on the Mind of the Primary Child. But what had these attainments got her? Eighteen hundred a year, plus a special responsibility allowance, and Peter Freake.

'Didn't your class mistress tell you that this isn't an ordinary firework party, but an artistic demonstration?' That was what she prepared to say, but changed her mind abruptly. If the little throw-back was kept in expectation he might behave decently for a while.

'The clowns will be along soon; really funny clowns, but they won't come unless you're a good boy, Peter.' She pronounced the lies without much conviction, but they succeeded and his face became eager. 'They're old clowns, nervous clowns and they don't like hooliganism. They only put on their show for good boys and girls.'

Eighteen

Tania had seen a man nailed to a wall. She had seen the faces of the people who had put him there and in spite of all the things they had done that brief revelation had aroused her pity. But though they were out of sight at the moment, she could still hear them and feel them and smell them. The mutter of cracked voices, the pressure of flagging muscles against the door, the stench of decay drifting through the gap in the frame. Tania had recognized the odour now, and the last time she had encountered it was when Mark showed her around a geriatric ward. It was the smell of approaching death – of sick, old people.

But everything was going to be all right. Quite all right, because she was not alone. She hadn't been able to move after she screamed. She had just stood there paralysed when they turned, staggered to their feet and shuffled towards her. Fear had held her as effectively as the chains which had held Elsie Kerr to the altar, and then suddenly she was free. Mark was beside her. He had rushed headlong down the stairs, he had slammed the door to blot out horror and as long as that door held she was all right – as right as rain – as right as ninepence – as right as right can be.

'Tania, you must do what I tell you.' Mark was struggling to keep a foothold on the stone floor. The door had only a spring catch and the pressure was increasing. The things behind the woodwork might be frail but there were at least thirty of them and one man and a woman could not resist their joint strength indefinitely. 'Go and get help. I told the police to meet me here, so find them. Run for help, darling.'

'Help – help – help!' Most of the creatures in the chapel were deaf, but a few ears had heard him. 'We are past help, but we know what his orders are – what we have to do. That you must go with us.'

'Run, Tania.' The pressure had relaxed, but a sudden blow jarred Mark's shoulder and he saw that one of the door panels was cracked. 'Find the police or look for something to wedge the door.'

'I can't leave you, Mark. You couldn't hold them on your own for a second.' There was another thud against the woodwork and Tania saw the crack widen to a gash. 'We've done all we can, so let's both run. Let's get away while there's a chance.'

'I can't, Tania. They mustn't get out ... I have to keep them there.' The pressure had returned and Mark gasped as he fought against it. He had only caught a brief glimpse of the room and its occupants, but it had been enough. The people behind the door were doomed both bodily and spiritually. They were dying – three of them appeared to be dead already: the poor tortured thing beside the altar, a woman slumped face-forward in a wheel-chair, a man who had not risen from his knees. But they all had to die where they were. Not one of them could be allowed to leave the chapel. 'Go for help, Tania.'

'I'm staying with you, Mark.' Tania's longing to run was stronger than any emotion she had experienced, but she realized that the self-sacrifice was justified. Also, though the blows were coming at regular intervals and the whole panel was splintering, the pressure seemed to be growing less and time was on their side.

She had not seen the final reels of the film, but she knew what they would have shown. Under the influence of drugs John Batterday had been forced to commit a final act of defiance against the Creator. He had raped a virgin on Satan's altar, and in the eyes of his captors that made him a demi-god, capable of passing on his longevity and supernatural powers to others.

But only after death, and the Wanderer was said to be death-less. Another ceremony had been needed to culminate the ritual. The panel had almost disintegrated, the voices behind it croaked triumphantly, but Tania shut her mind to them and once again she never heard the sounds above her. 'When thou art by men more evil than thyself consumed.' That was how a medieval troubadour reported the promise and that promise had been fulfilled. No animals had touched John Batterday's corpse; the pigs' instincts had saved them, but Tania knew how he had died. A eucharist had been celebrated and the host partaken.

The panel had a gaping hole, she could see the flash of metal as the base of an altar candle axed the hole wider, and soon a hand would appear; the hand of a communicant.

'*Hoc est enim corpus meum* . . . This is my body which is given for you.' Gods are not merely divine – they are food; manna to pass on eternal life. The bread and the wine, the water and the word, the flesh and the blood; that was how the Wandering Jew had found release. The weak would have used hatchets and knives, the strong their teeth. Human beings had gnawed the body of Buttadaeus while he was still alive.

There was the hand coming through the hole now, just as she had pictured it; crooked as a talon, wizened and grey like a monkey's paw. A nightmare sliding out through the shattered timber with fingernails outstretched to claw at her. It was touching her sleeve and Tania knew that she and Mark were beaten. Her arms left the door and she drew back in blind panic, seeing Mark do the same, though he had a different reason.

The arm of the law had made their arms unnecessary, the door was secure and the hand had vanished as a rolled overcoat of regulation blue serge was thrust against the hole and the voice of authority rasped down the stairs.

'All right, Levin, we'll take over,' said Commander Roland Trant.

'Clowns – there's going to be clowns.' Miss Yard's lie had fallen on fertile ground and the news was spreading.

'Who said so?' . . . 'Peter Freake of Class Four did.' . . . 'Then I don't believe yer, because he's a ruddy liar.' . . . 'Neither do I. If it was Monday, he'd tell you it's Sunday, Peter Freake would.'

'I hope it's true, though. I'd lub to see some clowns.' One of the group had adenoids and found it difficult to pronounce his v's. 'Clowns'd liben things up, eh – lubberly clowns.' As the teachers had said, the display was intended to have artistic merit, but it was too artistic for many of the audience. One firework is pretty much like another and they had been getting restive till the promise of further entertainment spread.

'It's true enough, though. I heard old Barnyard tell Peter there'd be clowns if he behaved himself. And he'd better behave, too, or I'll sling him in the river.'

'Me too. I want to see them clowns, but where are they – which way will they come?'

'Over the water, maybe. Cor, it would be a lark if they came across on stilts. Can't you just imagine that?'

'I'll say I can, so let's watch Peter and see he don't do nothing to annoy Barnyard. We don't want her stoppin' them clowns, do we? We want to see their show; lubberly . . . lubberly . . . lubberly clowns.'

Nineteen

'Where the hell is that decontamination squad that I asked Plunket to send over?' Mark looked at his watch. The lights in the chapel had gone out when Trant and his three constables appeared on the staircase and there had been curses and shuffles, but that was a quarter of an hour ago. Now apart from a grunting, moaning sound, they had heard nothing from behind the door for the last ten minutes.

'A squad might take time to organize, Sir Marcus, and in the meanwhile we can't just stand here.' The Commander took a torch from his pocket and motioned to the man holding the coat against the broken panel. 'I'll take a look, Constable Elliot.'

'No, please stay where you are.' Tania imagined that clawlike hand poised in the darkness. 'When they ran that film they were praying for orders, and I know what those orders will be. But the room's a cellar and they're trapped. As long as the door's sealed there's nothing to worry about.'

'But we must do something. Whatever crimes those people have committed, they're still human beings, suffering from a terrible illness. You're a doctor, Sir Marcus, and surely you can help them in some way?'

'I'm afraid my wife's correct, Commander.' Mark looked at his medical bag lying on the floor. 'Those people are doomed; most of them may be dead already, and they're past human help. They must have known that themselves when they heard Aikenhead's first statement. They hoped to gain immortality and spiritual power by eating a man's body and the process worked the opposite way. The cells responsible for Batterday's own longevity destroyed their glandular balance and they are dying of precocious old age: "Rampant Progeria".'

'But surely something can be done for them?' The policeman was clearly distressed by the moans which were growing fainter. 'Shots of morphine, perhaps?'

'Don't be a fool, Mr Trant.' He had taken a step forward and Mark gripped his arm. 'When they were in normal health those people dedicated themselves to the service of the devil and I don't think they'll desert their master now. At the moment they will have only one ambition and . . .'

'Ambition?' Trant pulled aside his arm. 'What ambition could anyone have at the point of death?'

'Companionship, of course. Their illness can probably be passed on by the saliva and quite certainly by any light scratch or graze that penetrates the skin. Every one of them still capable of thought will be praying for us to open that door and give them the chance to spread the disease.' Mark thought of a historical example to explain his reasoning. 'It's a common enough phenomenon. During the great plague of London Samuel Pepys wrote that "ill people would breathe in the faces of well people passing by." Breathe deliberately, Commander.'

'I suppose you're right.' Trant lowered the torch reluctantly. 'But that damn noise is getting me down.'

'It's getting all of us down, but the decontamination unit must be along soon and they'll have protective clothing and masks. Then something can be done.'

'There may be a delay, sir.' One of the policemen had a radio headphone against his left ear. 'If they were coming from St Bede's the vans would take the Ladysmith Road route and there's a bad hold-up. A lorry jack-knifed on the roundabout apparently.'

'I see.' Mark's face became as rigid as a graven image. The moans had distressed him as much as Trant, but they had stopped now and the complete silence beyond the door disturbed him even more deeply. Three people had died, but what about the rest? He had imagined them stationed around the door waiting to strike their last blow against mankind, but others must be feeling the approach of death by now and its sound should be audible. 'You are quite sure the room was a cellar and this was its only exit, Tania?'

'I assumed so, though there was a curtain across one wall so I can't be completely certain. But I am sure they'll never leave the room. It's their chapel and they want to die there.

'What are you going to do, Mark?' He had held out his hand for Trant's torch and she stepped in front of him. 'You can't go in there. You know what might happen better than anyone.'

'I'm not going in anywhere, but I must take a quick look.' The door was securely wedged at the base and Mark motioned the man holding the coat to step aside. 'And don't worry, darling. I had a million units of Genomycin pumped into me last night and they should have given my system immunity by now.' Was that true, he wondered as he pushed past her and moved towards the door. The antibiotic would kill the infection after a period; Elsie Kerr's symptoms had proved that, but how long would that period be? Would the pituitary suffer irreparable damage before the alien cells died? He was probably about to commit suicide, but the risk had to be taken and his affairs were in order. He had made his will, his conscience was fairly clear, and Tania was a young and attractive woman who would find another husband.

Mark screened his mouth and nostrils with a handkerchief and raised the torch to the broken panel, but all he could see was an expanse of wall and he forced himself to draw closer and put his eyes to the hole itself, waiting for that wizened hand to reappear – waiting to feel the slash of fingernails and hear the croak of senile laughter which would follow.

But at the beginning there was no movement and no sound at all. The torch beam swept around the chapel and the first thing he saw was an old woman slumped in a wheelchair. She was clearly dead, as was the man hanging beside the altar and another man kneeling near the huge marble figure of his deity. No grotesque or obscene representation which might have appeared in John Batterday's collection, but the supreme lie. The dark angel crowned and triumphant with a smoking lamp in one hand, a chalice in the other, while behind the image pictures glorified the master's ceremonials. Mark recognized the blood sacrifices of Adonis and Osiris, the mutilation of Attis and the ritual slaughter of the Mexican god-kings. But he only looked at them briefly, because he was suddenly terrified, though there was nothing in the room to cause him physical harm. It was the statue that frightened him: Satan was not an image, he was alive and his features were moving.

For perhaps five seconds Mark's eyes were rooted on the phe- nomenon and then he drew back with a curse as he realized its cause. Smoke from the lamp was blowing in gusts across the stone features to produce the illusion and the air creating those gusts came from an open window that curtains had once screened. And not only air, sound came too; the phut-phut-phut of a motorboat heading away from its moorings.

He swung round and shouted to the policemen to open the door. The room was no cellar, as Tania imagined, but a basement with an exit facing the river. The witches were not all dead, they had flown. They were free to carry out their master's orders for a little longer and soon, 'Ill people would breathe in the faces of well people passing by.'

He might be middle-aged, he and Tania were both dog-tired, but they had outpaced the police. Mark let in the clutch before Trant and his constables reached their car and sent Paul Johnston's souped-up Mini hurtling from the kerb.

It was a pleasant evening – the sky clear over London, the tide high, the moon up – and the launch came into sight as he swung the little car on to a road running parallel to the river. The boat looked completely inoffensive in the distance, and so did its occu- pants. They might have been a partly of anglers returning home from a fishing expedition, or tourists viewing the night life of Old Father Thames. Tania had once made such a trip and she almost seemed to hear the guide's voice drifting towards them across the water.

'On your right, Southwark – the probable site of Shakespeare's

Globe Theatre, and to the left the Tower constructed by William the Conquerer during the years ... after passing the next bridge we will enter the Pool of London, and then put in for refreshments at the Prospect of Whitby; a historic inn, against the walls of which pirates were once chained to await drowning by the tide.'

Chains! Little Elsie Kerr had been chained. The memory returned Tania to present reality and she looked at the launch with a shudder. They were not following a fishing boat or pleasure craft and its crew were not anglers or tourists. They were blights, spreaders of sickness, sailing down London's river with cargoes to ravage their fellow men.

'Trant must have contacted the Thames police by now, and if only they reach them in time.' Mark considered how the operation might be done. 'They could get a grapple on that boat and keep it towed away from the shore. Even half an hour would be sufficient. They're dying, darling; dying quickly. Where they're concerned minutes count as years, so please God they die before finding a place to land.'

'They'll look for somewhere that's crowded, of course.' The car was abreast of the boat now and Mark slowed down. A place where there were plenty of people to receive their gifts, he thought. People enjoying themselves ... having a good time ... going about their business ... queuing near an embankment for theatres or buses or taxis. People who would have no fear of the audacious old men and women coming ashore from their expedition. On the contrary, they'd be full of admiration and eager to assist. 'Grab hold of my arm. Dad, and I'll help you ashore. Hold on tight, dear; we'll see you don't fall.'

'Mark, there's a landing-stage ahead.' Tania had been watching the lights. The moonlight with a flock of birds circling beneath it; wild geese – great, grey barnacle geese which she had never seen in England before. House lights and street lights, rockets in the sky, the lights of the police car following them, a swirling blaze of light from a battery of Catherine wheels. 'They're letting off fireworks, darling, and I can see people: hundreds of them; hundreds of children.'

'Brace yourself, Tania.' The road was forking away from the

river, a concrete post blocked the tow-path and a sign on a wall stated that the lane ahead was prohibited to motor vehicles. The police Jaguar could never squeeze through the gap, but a Mini might. Though Mark had no idea what he and Tania could accomplish on their own, his foot came down on the accelerator.

He had seen the crowd along the bank, and the people on the launch had seen it too. The bows were swinging inshore and somehow they had to be stopped. Henson's little craft had no nuclear propellant, no rockets or warheads, but it was quite as deadly as any Polaris submarine – a Pandora's box full of mischief to plague the earth.

'Here they come.' . . . 'Clowns.' . . . 'Clowns.' . . . 'Lovely.' . . . 'Lubberly clowns.' Not only Mark and Tania had seen the launch turn towards the bank, and when a firework lit up the faces of its passengers, the reception was rapturous.

'Who's calling me a liar, now? Told you there'd be clowns, didn't I? Said old Barny had promised us clowns.' Peter Freake was yelling at the top of his voice. 'And they're right good uns, ain't they? Look at those jossers at the tiller . . . see how they're made up to look old . . . Cor, they might be a hundred years each.'

'They're bloody marvellous, Pete; all of 'em are.' . . . 'Good for Barnyard.' . . . 'Better than any circus clowns, I've seen.' His companions were leaping up and down against the rope barrier in their excitement. 'Much better.' . . . 'Best clowns in the world, ours are.' . . . 'Our clowns – our very own clowns.' . . . 'Our funny, ugly, old river clowns.'

Twenty

'Get out of the way, damn you.' The Mini had squeezed through the gap between the post and the wall at the cost of a buckled front wing, but a car was no more use to Mark and Tania. The route to the water was blocked by hundreds of wildly excited children.

'Let us pass.' Mark fought against the crush, elbowing shoulders, tugging at arms and cuffing heads, but he made slow progress because the children were completely out of control. They'd never seen such realistic clowns. Such wonderfully funny old clowns who were much, much more entertaining than any silly fireworks.

'Look at the bloke steerin' . . . like old what's-his-name in the bible – Methuselah.' . . . 'Like an Egyptian mummy.' . . . 'Like a great, skinny ape dressed up like a human being.' Till recently Professor Henson had been a stout man, but that was some hours ago. He was as thin now as the living corpses Mark had seen at Belsen, and his suit hung around his wasted body like sacking.

'What about the old girl on the right, though? Ain't she something? Look how her wig's comin' adrift.' The housewife had once been extremely proud of her auburn hair, but she was almost bald and the breeze was tearing away the few white strands that remained to her.

'See that crusher in the black coat.' Henson's manservant was still on duty beside his master. It took all their failing energies to hold the launch on course, but they were both smiling. With the exception of the photographer, who was in his death throes, and two corpses stretched out on deck, the whole boatload were smiling and waving greetings. Thin lips drawn back to reveal blackened teeth or toothless gums, and their wizened hands flapping at the children. In a few minutes they were going to die, but they would have companions to follow them on the long journey.

'Give the blighters a song – show 'em that we like their act. They're river clowns – water clowns, so what about the Volga Boatman? "Sons of the river – Pulling together – Yo-heave-ho." '

'For God's sake let me get through.' The launch was still over forty yards from the steps, Mark had approximately half that distance to go, but high above him the circling geese honked and screamed as if in mockery and the children's voices drowned his demands. 'Yo, heave-ho . . . Yo, heave-ho . . .'

The last time Mark had heard that chant was in Poland and the year had been 1941. The day on which the Russian occupation forces withdrew from Lemberg and an SS regiment marched in. The day when he had started on his travels – to the Ruhr labour camps and the camp at Belsen-Bergen – to London, where he'd got his degree, and to Oxford and New York where he won his fellowships – to Vietnam where Rachel, his first wife, had died – to East Germany where he met Tania. Before he ever knew his *Doppelgänger*, John Batterday, Mark had sometimes mocked himself in terms of the legend; a wandering Hebrew, a hiking kike, a yid with a yen to travel. During some of those journeys he had imagined he had witnessed the worst abominations that the dark angel, the Fallen Star of the Morning, could devise.

How wrong! How bloody foolish he had been! Tania was far behind him, lost in the crush of bodies and the teachers' discipline had gone to pieces. The rope barrier had been broken or untied, the children were jostling down the steps to the water's edge and the launch was coming in. He could see its occupants clearly at last. See the smiling faces above the gaunt bodies, see the matchstick arms raised in greeting with fingernails poised to slash and stab. He knew what the verbal greetings would be. 'Give us a hand ashore, lad.' . . . 'Put up your face and let Gran kiss you, dearie.'

'Out of the way!' He had reached the top of the steps, but the going was even harder and his fists slammed out in desperation. He saw blood spurt from the face of a small girl and he heard her scream as she crashed back on to the concrete path. He might have maimed her for life, the fall could even have killed her, and in his mind a saying he had once derided joined the Volga Boat Song. 'Pulling together . . . Sons of the River . . . Any man's death diminishes me.'

'Children, come back from the steps.' Trant's driver had found a way round to the embankment and the car's loudspeaker blared over the crowd. 'I am a police officer and that is an order. The people in that boat are dangerous, and you must, *must* keep away from them.'

Trant might have been talking to stones for all the attention he received, and Mark started to fight his way down the stairs. The launch was very close and behind it an unladen petrol barge had emerged from a bend of the river, its raised propellers creaming the water.

Step by step Mark struggled forward to meet the beings who would soon be entering the inner core of hell, and while he did so, a police searchlight lit up the name Henson had given his boat. *Dolores*; a common Spanish name, which made one think of holidays and flamenco dancing and a film star of the 'thirties called Dolores del Rio. But also of sadness and one of the most perverse poems in the English language.

'O mystic and sombre Dolores, Our Lady of Pain.' Though he was gasping for breath, Mark quoted aloud because pain was very near to him. The insignificant pain of a scratch at first; the revulsion of spittle spraying his face, but the horrible pangs of old age would follow. The heart weakening, arteries growing hard, lungs labouring. He might experience the symptoms soon, because the launch was almost up to the bank and its occupants were shuffling forward to disembark. And with them came the odours that had been present in the chapel: the stench of sulphur and incense clinging to their clothes and the smell of their bodies; sickness, incontinence, approaching death.

Rampant progeria – precocious old age – 'Old Father Thames keeps rolling along, down to the mighty sea.' The song had changed, but not all the children were singing. Those on the lower steps had realized what Mark was up to. They knew that he was trying to spoil the fun and stop their comical friends landing – to prevent those lubberly old clowns coming ashore to perform for them. They wouldn't have that – they'd hold him back. Small, wiry fingers tugged at his clothes, determined little bodies barred his way, hands clutched his arms, a head thudded into his side, a leg shot out and he tripped and toppled forward.

He was there, though. He had fallen on to the last step, with the water lapping his knees, and he reached out to meet the impact of the launch. Young voices abused him as a spoilsport, old voices screeched and cursed at him, but he somehow made it. His palms were against the boat's prow and his body had become a bridge – a barrier to protect the children.

A barrier which would soon be crushed, because he couldn't stop the launch for more than a few seconds. The thrust of the motor was too strong for him, and all he could do was pray for a miracle and fight on to the bitter end.

A very bitter end, and there was no hope of avoiding it. The hands on the tiller belonged to dying men, but they were keeping the bows pointed at the steps and the pressure was buckling his spine. And other hands were about to hasten his defeat. An old man had lifted a boathook and was pointing it at him like a lance. An old woman was leaning forward with fingers outstretched to tear at his eyeballs; long, thin fingers covered with rings that slipped over her knuckles as she prepared to claim him for a companion. He saw an engagement ring, a wedding ring and an eternity ring falling from fleshless hands that had recently belonged to a buxom, middle-aged woman. Rings that glinted in the moonlight and then vanished under the water.

And those rings were the last things Mark saw for a long time. The boathook struck home, blood poured from his forehead to obscure his eyes, and he knew he was about to faint. But just before losing consciousness, he heard Tania's voice and wondered why she was shouting in a mixture of English and German. 'The birds . . . the Gabriel Hounds . . . *die sieben Pfeifer.*'

That was Mark's final experience till he came to in the hospital; he never saw the geese attack. The Seven Whistlers, Batterday's avengers, swooping out of the sky like dogs after a quarry. Strong, grey wings beating frail hands from the tiller, serpent-like necks flailing, beaks tearing human flesh. He never saw the boat swing round and lurch towards the petrol tanker. He didn't hear the crash when the tanker's bows split open the hull or the screams as its propellers crushed the dying bodies. He just lay on the step with the water lapping his face and when, much later, Tania explained what happened he was at a loss for words.

That irritated him. For the first time in years Sir Marcus Levin, K.C.B., F.R.S. and Nobel Prizewinner, didn't know what to say and it was a situation he disliked. But there was a phrase, an appropriate quotation which fitted in with what Tania had told him and he had used it only a few days ago before a class of students.

Just how did the saying go? Something about someone, some person or thing acting in some unorthodox manner to carry out some task.

No, that wasn't quite right, though he was getting warm. Not 'acting' – not 'manner' – not 'unorthodox' – not 'task'. He'd have to think again.

'Please let me concentrate, Brian.' Plunket was telling him to try to sleep, but how could he relax till he'd remembered the exact words? 'Something . . . some force . . . somebody moving in a mysterious way his wonders to perform.'